HOLLOW JUSTICE

THE COWBOY JUSTICE ASSOCIATION
BOOK THIRTEEN

by Olivia James

www.OliviaJaymes.com

CHAPTER ONE

Mornings in the Monroe household were often hectic as four people, one dog, and a cat named Charlie all descended on the kitchen at once, trying to get ready for the day ahead. There was breakfast, of course, and during the school year there would be lunches to pack, instruments for band, equipment for soccer practice, not to mention books and homework that had to be stuffed into overflowing backpacks.

In the summer it was slightly less hectic, so they only had to pack lunches and make sure each child was covered in sunscreen from head to toe. Today the summer camp that the children attended was having a field day so Lizzie and Nate would come back dirty, sweaty, and exhausted.

Jared loved the controlled chaos even when he hadn't yet had his first cup of coffee. He'd grown up in a house full of people, so this wasn't anything out of the ordinary for him. His wife Misty, on the other hand, was an only child of a single parent. No other relatives, either. Her home had been significantly quieter than his own, and less busy. He'd assured her several times that this was normal but more than once she'd doubted him.

"Let's have two," Misty whispered into his ear as their daughter Lizzie and their son Nathaniel said goodbye to the dog before they left for summer day camp. "It'll be great. We can handle it. That's what you said. You said having two would be no more different than having one. You lied to me, Jared Monroe."

She teased him about this on occasion. It was true that he'd been the first one to bring up having a second child, but she'd eagerly agreed, telling him that she'd been thinking about it as well. But he'd gladly say it was all his idea when they had a rough night or morning. Last night, Nate had a nightmare, so he'd ended up crawling into bed with them along with Stevie, their Golden Retriever.

The canine was named "Stevie" because Nate had wanted to name it Captain America, but they'd vetoed that, so he'd started calling him "Steve" for "Steve Rogers." They'd tried explaining to Nate that "Steve" was actually a girl but he didn't care. Misty had somehow convinced him to change it to "Stevie" so when anyone questioned her about it she could say that the dog was named after Stevie Nicks, the singer from Fleetwood Mac.

Although they had a California King bed, two adults, one child, and one dog took up every bit of space so neither he nor Misty had slept well last night. Nate and Stevie? They'd slept fine. Charlie the cat slept on a purple and gold throne in Lizzie's room, as befitting his station in the household.

"I did lie," he agreed, taking another deep gulp of his coffee. He had a busy day at the office ahead and he needed the caffeine. "But I don't think you're that upset about it, to be truthful."

Her eyes sparkled with mischief and he suddenly wished that they were alone, upstairs in their bedroom. His wife was absolutely drop dead gorgeous, even after all these years and two kids. He'd often tease her about having made a deal with the devil because she seriously didn't look a day older than when they'd married.

Today she looked particularly fetching in an old, worn-out pair jeans that molded her luscious backside and a white tank top that clung to all the right places. His Misty wasn't a tall woman, instead petite and dainty, almost pixie-ish. She still had her long, pale blonde hair, and although he would have been fine if she'd cut it, he was secretly thrilled that she never had. If she'd told him that the only way she'd keep it was that he had to wash it every single day? He'd take that deal.

He was on the wrong side of forty but still head over heels for his wife, like a teenager in love with his first crush. Luckily, he was pretty damn sure that she felt the same. Their marriage wasn't always easy, but it was well worth it.

"I'm not all that upset," she admitted, stuffing her sunglasses and lip balm into her purse. She had to take the kids to camp and then run some errands. "Are you going to be late tonight? Should I cook or order in?"

"I'll pick up dinner on my way home. And I won't be late," he promised, leaning down to press a quick kiss to her full pink lips. Lizzie and Nate made gagging noises in the background. They did that every time he and Misty showed any affection for each other. Which was quite a lot. "Italian, okay?"

He could get a variety of dishes and they could all share.

"Sounds perfect. Thanks for picking up dinner. I have a meeting with the gallery this morning and then I'm taking Charlie to the vet for his shots. You know how much he likes that."

For the most part Charlie was as lazy and laid back as the day was long, but he didn't like the vet at all, hissing at him every single time.

"He's going to hate us afterward."

"What's this *us* stuff?" Misty groaned. "He's going to hate me because I was the one who took him. He'll love up on you tonight and give me the cold shoulder."

"I'll take one for the team and tell him it was my idea."

"Sure, that'll work." Misty slung her purse over her shoulder. "Okay, are you ready for camp? Lunches? Water bottles?"

They went through this every day and yet at least once a week one of the kids would forget something that they desperately needed. Jared was sure that he didn't remember being like that but if his parents were alive, they'd probably tell him differently.

That pang in the region of his heart. It still hurt to think about his father's passing, just six months ago. A heart attack had taken the family patriarch, but in many ways Gerald Monroe had been gone for a long time, his memories and dignity robbed by Alzheimer's. At least now his father was with his beloved wife. At the end, his father hadn't remembered Jared, but he'd talked about his spouse. He'd ask for her constantly. They'd had a life-long love affair to be envied.

Following his family out to the garage, he helped load the kids and their backpacks into the minivan and then gave his beautiful wife another quick kiss.

"You got something on your mind, handsome?" she whispered playfully in his ear. "Two kisses this morning? I usually only get one."

"You can have as many as you like, and yes, I do have something on my mind. Meet you upstairs in bed about ten o'clock tonight? I'll bring the wine."

She gave his hand a squeeze. "It's a date."

He watched as Misty backed down the driveway and pulled out onto the road before he climbed into his own vehicle and headed for the office. He didn't go in every single day as a good portion of his work could be done at home, but he had a meeting with his partners, Logan Wright and Jason Anderson, and he wanted to be in person for it.

The office was mostly deserted when he showed up, but the coffee was already made and hot. Logan had probably done that, which meant that the brew would be industrial strength. He poured himself a cup and added plenty of sugar and cream, and then headed straight for Jason's office. Logan was sitting on the sofa against the wall drinking his coffee and munching on a cruller while Jason was kicked back in his big leather chair, cowboy boots up on the mahogany desktop. Like he owned the whole goddamn world instead of just a huge chunk of Montana.

"There better be a chocolate frosted in that box of pastries," Jared warned, throwing himself down into an overstuffed chair. "That's the only thing that made it worth commuting into the office for today."

Logan pushed the box closer to Jared. "There is because I knew you'd whine like a little girl if there wasn't."

"Jesus, you two act like kids most of the time," Jason huffed, swinging his legs down to the floor. "Can you try to act over eighteen for at least a few minutes?"

"I can try," Jared grunted, stuffing his face with the sugared confection. "But I make no promises."

"Sometimes I feel sorry for Misty," Jason lamented with a chuckle. "That poor woman."

Logan laughed and reached for another donut. "I feel sorry for all our wives. We're all a bunch of trouble, let's face it. They're saints to deal with us."

Saint might be taking it a step too far, but their wives were wonderful and extremely patient people.

Really, really patient.

Jared had shit to do, although hanging out with his two best friends and eating pastries wouldn't be a bad way to spend the day. It just wouldn't be all that productive.

"So what's on the agenda?" he asked Jason.

"Budgets," his friend answered. "Upcoming vacation scheduling, and we also need to discuss the serials and stalkers unit."

Discussing the budget was never fun but it had to be done. They were doing far better than they'd ever dreamed when they'd first opened the consulting firm. Back then it had simply been an idea, but they'd hadn't known if small towns would truly use their services. It might have all been a pipe dream that could have come crashing down in an ugly way.

Years later, it was all different. Only a portion of their revenue came in from small towns utilizing their services. Some of it came from mid-sized cities and the rest came from private citizens hiring them to augment their local police in active and cold cases. They hadn't set out to service the public, but as the business had grown so had their client base.

They made quick work of the budgeting discussion, agreeing to buy some new computer equipment and to also hire another administrative person to deal with the day to day hassle of running an office and keeping it stocked with coffee, pens, and toilet paper. The vacation schedule took slightly longer as they all three pulled out their calendars and marked off the days during the holidays that they wanted off.

The task force discussion was even faster, as they all agreed that to be fully staffed it needed four, not two full-time permanent people. That meant that all of the candidates, currently working on a trial basis, were going to make the team after all. They'd reassess in six months to see if any additional resources would be needed.

After the meeting, Jared went back into his office and closed the door so he could get some heads down work done. It was a few hours later when his coffee cup was empty and his shoulders were screaming to be stretched that he heard a knock at his door.

"Come in."

Tracy, their administrative assistant, poked her head in. "There's a man out here asking for you. Says he works for a law firm – Dwight, Michaels, and Baker. He says it's important."

It was rare that anyone asked for Jared personally as he was mostly behind the scenes, dealing with the computer research, the business, and the staff. Jason and Logan did most of the public work, putting their faces out there while Jared stayed in the shadows. The arrangement suited him fine.

"Send him in, I guess. But in about ten minutes remind me that I have an appointment, okay?"

"Got it."

Rising from his chair, Jared shook hands with the younger man that Tracy ushered in. He couldn't be older than thirty, his features rather boyish. He was dressed in a dark blue suit and carried a brown leather briefcase.

"Jared Monroe? I'm Bradley Baker of Dwight, Michaels, and Baker. Thank you for seeing me."

Jared made a mental note to research the law firm. Was Bradley a partner at this young age?

"No problem, please have a seat." They both sat down, Baker balancing his briefcase on his knees. "What can I do for you?"

"I won't take up much of your time," the other man assured him with a smile. "I'm actually here to drop off a letter for your wife, Misty Foster Monroe."

Misty?

"Is she being sued, Mr. Baker?"

The man's brows flew up and then he vigorously shook his head. "No, not at all. I'm sorry. I guess I should start at the beginning."

"That would be a good idea."

"My firm represents a man that would like to reach out and contact your wife. This letter explains it in detail."

Baker fumbled with the latch on the case and then pulled out a flat, white legal-sized envelope. Misty's name was written on it in block print letters.

"A man? Who wants to contact my wife?" Jared didn't like the sound of this at all. He was about five seconds from showing Bradley Baker the door. "Who is this person and what does he want?"

"Well...it's all in the letter."

Baker held it out, a hopeful smile on his face. Jared cleared his throat and leaned forward, wanting his visitor to understand just how serious he was about anything to do with his spouse.

"If you want me to take this envelope and give it to my wife, I'm going to need a little more to go on. I'll ask once again. Who is this person and what do they want with Misty?"

Nervously fussing with his tie, Baker placed the envelope on the edge of the desk. "The person is Adam Reynolds."

"Never heard of him."

"He owns several large companies, including the Chipper Shopper chain."

There was a Chipper Shopper store in pretty much every town west of the Mississippi.

"What does Adam Reynolds want with my wife?"

Misty's reputation as an artist had been growing these last several years. Perhaps he wanted to commission a piece of art from her. This was a strange way to go about it, however. Most people contacted her through her website or her agent.

Baker coughed, his palm pressed against his chest.

"Mr. Reynolds believes that your wife Misty is his daughter."

Her father? Jared hadn't been expecting this.

"Then I think I have a few more questions."

CHAPTER TWO

Misty wasn't a suspicious woman by nature, and her husband Jared had certainly never given her any reason to be one, either. But tonight something was different. She couldn't quite put her finger on it, but Jared was acting strangely.

He'd barely paid attention to anyone this evening during dinner, his gaze off in the distance, his mind heaven knew where. He was the type that liked to dive deeply into his job and at times he could become distracted, almost obsessed, but she'd never minded. She could be that way as well.

Nate had asked his dad twice so far if they were going to play catch outside in the backyard and Jared had yet to answer him. It looked like he wasn't even paying any attention. Finally, Nate grabbed onto the cuff of his father's button-down shirt and gave it a tug.

"Dad, are you listening to me?"

Jerking his head toward his son, Jared sighed. "No, I wasn't listening. I'm sorry. Please tell me again."

Nate repeated his question and Jared responded affirmatively that they absolutely were going to play catch after dinner, but they wouldn't have too long as the sun would be down soon.

Now that Jared was engaged with his children, Lizzie regaled him with all the things she'd done at camp that day and he listened intently, nodding and replying in all the right places.

His head isn't in the game, though. I can tell.

Misty had learned many years ago that Jared wasn't a man that easily talked. Silence was his most comfortable state, although he'd loosened up quite a bit since their marriage. Still, it was hard to get him to give voice to his problems and concerns. His father Gerald Monroe had been a wonderful man whom Misty had adored, but unfortunately, he'd instilled in his sons that men suffered in silence. Any other way wasn't masculine.

Her husband knew that wasn't true but long-ingrained habits were hard to break. He had something on his mind and hopefully, once they were alone, she could get him to talk about it.

After dinner, he'd quickly helped her load the dishwasher and then went outside with both of the kids. Misty took the opportunity to soak in a hot bath for a few minutes before dressing in a pair of soft flannel pajama bottoms and t-shirt. It was Jared's night to get the kids ready for bed, but it was her turn to read to them. They were working through the Harry Potter series and they'd recently started book three, which was Misty's favorite.

"You know what flannel does to me," Jared teased when they were finally alone in their bedroom. Lizzie and Nate had fallen asleep and with any luck would stay that way until morning. "It's not fair that you're so sexy."

Misty would have argued that it was even more not fair that Jared looked better and better as he aged. What was it about a man with a touch of silver in his hair and some lines around his eyes? He still had women flirting with him everywhere he went. Jared being Jared, he rarely noticed.

Lounging back on her pillows, she stretched out her legs to show off her plaid pajama pants. "You should really see someone about that fetish, Jared Monroe. You're a sick man."

"But you love me anyway."

She did. More than she'd ever thought she could. Before him she'd assumed that she'd be alone, but then he'd thundered and stomped into her life and things had never been the same.

Thank goodness.

"I do," she confirmed. "But the flannel thing is still weird."

"I can live with it." He hadn't moved from where he was standing in the middle of the bedroom. Normally, he'd either be romancing her on the bed or heading into the bathroom for a quick shower. He wasn't doing either of those things, simply standing there and looking at her as if she had the secrets of the universe.

Spoiler alert–she didn't, and he knew that. He had something on his mind for sure. Maybe a nudge would help him open up?

"Did anything interesting happen at work today? I know you had a meeting with Jason and Logan."

Budgets, if she remembered correctly. Perhaps business wasn't booming as much as it had been. Was he worried about money? He never had before but there was always a first time.

Jared didn't answer immediately, which had Misty even more curious as to what was going on with her husband. He rarely ducked a direct question.

"Yes, something happened at work today."

Okay, progress.

"Do you want to talk about it? Is there a problem with the business?" A nasty thought occurred to her and she sat straight up, her heart lurching in her chest. "Is everyone alright? Is someone sick?"

His brows shot up and he vigorously shook his head. "No,

not at all. Everyone's fine. Shit, I'm not doing this very well."

Sighing in relief, Misty fell back against the pillows. "I can't say whether you are or aren't as I have no clue what it is that you're trying to do."

Reaching into his pocket, he pulled out a white, legal-sized envelope folded in half. "This came for you today at the office."

She took it from his outstretched hand and examined the item that was clearly bothering her spouse. It looked innocent enough. Her name was on the outside of it, printed in block letters, but there was nothing else. It was sealed, however, so he couldn't have read the contents.

Then why is he acting so strangely?

"An attorney brought it," Jared explained as she turned the envelope over in her hands, studying it. "It's from Adam Reynolds."

Frowning, she dragged her gaze from the letter to her husband. "Adam Reynolds? Why does that name sound familiar?"

"He owns Chipper Shopper plus a myriad of other investments, including a hell of a lot of real estate and land."

"Does he want to commission me? He should go through my agent."

"He doesn't want a piece of art, honey."

She held up the envelope. "Then what does he want?"

Jared rubbed the back of his neck, a grimace contorting his handsome features.

"Apparently, Adam Reynolds thinks he's your father."

Of all the things that could have come out of Jared's mouth, those words were the last that she had expected.

It simply couldn't be true.

"I think you better start from the beginning and tell me every detail."

✧   ✧   ✧   ✧

Misty had listened to Jared's explanation of his meeting with the attorney. Twice. She still wasn't sure that it was real. It couldn't be. Her own mother had told her that she didn't know who Misty's father was. She'd always said that it didn't matter because the two of them were a team. A dad would only be in the way. For the longest time, Misty had believed that and when she was older it didn't matter that much anyway. She didn't miss what she'd never had.

"So you didn't read what was inside?"

He'd come to lie next to her in bed, pulling her against the warmth of his body.

"I would never read your mail."

"It's not real federal government mail. It's an envelope."

"With your name on it. Would you have opened it if the situation was reversed?"

She wrinkled her nose in thought. "Maybe. I'm not sure. If I thought I was protecting you I might. I don't know. It's sealed, so if I did open it I wouldn't be keeping that from you."

"Do you want me to open it?"

A part of her did. Just hand him the letter and let him deal with it. Not the most mature reaction she'd ever had.

"Yes, but I'm going to do it myself anyway because I don't want to think that I'm that chicken shit."

"Listen, you don't have to open it. You can just shove it in a drawer and pretend it didn't happen. Maybe open it down the road. You have the choice here."

"I do have the choice," she agreed. "I don't have to open it. I could just rip it up or burn it."

She could... Then go back to her idyllic existence, none the wiser about the Pandora's Box she currently held in her hands. Opening and reading the letter could change everything, and she wasn't sure that she wanted anything to be changed. She liked her life just the way it was. She was happy and deliriously in love. She had two beautiful children and a lovely home. They were all healthy, too. There wasn't anything that a long-lost father could add to her life. It didn't matter what this Adam Reynolds person had to say. And where the hell had he been anyway when she and her mother had struggled for food on the table? He hadn't been a father then when she'd really needed him. She didn't need him now.

Screw him. He was decades too late. She wasn't going to let some asshole billionaire mess up her happy life.

"I don't need this or him. I'm just going to throw it away."

It landed in the empty trash can next to the bed within seconds. Decision made. She could move forward now. Looking back was a waste of time.

She didn't need Adam Reynolds or anything he might have to offer.

"I can't believe you did that. You just tossed it in the garbage?"

The next morning Misty was sitting on the couch while talking on the phone with her best friend Rayne. Jared had left for work and she'd dropped the kids at camp before starting a load of laundry and washing the breakfast dishes. She'd wanted some studio time to work but her mind was still on the letter that was sitting in the trash can upstairs. She hated that it was bugging her, so to get her mind off of it she called Rayne.

"What was I supposed to do with it? He's a little late, don't you think?"

"Well…yes, but maybe there are reasons. You won't know if you don't open it."

"You'd open it?"

"I couldn't help myself," Rayne declared. "The mystery

would make me crazy. I'd have to read it eventually. Aren't you even a little curious about this man that thinks he might be your father? Just a little?"

"Sure…but…I don't need a father in my life at this juncture. What would I even say to him? I don't even really know if he is my father."

"They have tests for that. A quick swab of your cheek and you could find out."

The test was that easy but the emotions surrounding it were far more complicated.

"I'm just not sure that I want to know. I've gone this long and it hasn't made a difference."

"Then you're a better person than I am. I couldn't *not* open that letter if only to see what he had to say."

That stupid letter was the reason Misty hadn't slept well last night. She was wishing that Jared had never given it to her.

"How could my mom even have met a man like Adam Reynolds?" Missy asked, her mind darting through her past trying to find even an inkling that her mother Annette might have given her. A stray remark. A name dropped in casual conversation. There was nothing. "He's a big shot CEO and she was poor and worked as a waitress. And if he's known all these years and didn't do anything, then he's a total bastard. Right?"

"I can't argue that," Rayne responded. "He would be an asshole, but you don't know the story."

And Misty wouldn't unless she opened that stupid envelope.

"I don't think a story exists that would make this scenario okay."

"So read the letter, and then send one back telling him what a horrible person he is. Get closure."

"I don't need closure. At least, I didn't need it until he sent that letter. This is really all his fault."

"If the letter is really bugging you and you don't want to read it, I have to ask this question then? Why haven't you burned or shredded it? You tossed it in the garbage can. You didn't rip it in half or anything. You simply threw it out inches from where you sleep. I might be crazy saying this but that doesn't sound like the action of a person that doesn't want to read it."

Dammit, Misty hated it when Rayne made sense.

Do I want to read it? Maybe. Kind of. I might want to.

"I think…I want the option to read it," Misty finally admitted. "If I want to, you know, at some point in the future."

"That's okay. Keep the letter. Shove it in the bottom of a drawer if you want. Jared was right. This is your choice. You can read it or not read it."

Rayne had a point. Misty had a choice. If she wasn't sure she wanted to read the letter or not, throwing it out might not be the best plan. It had been a knee-jerk reaction last night but in the cold light of day…

"I can't help but wonder what my mother would say about it."

"I can't answer that," Rayne replied. "What do you think she'd say?"

Annette had been a free spirit, not caring what anyone thought about her. She'd lived her life until the end with a passion that frankly Misty could only admire. Never once had her mother apologized for the decisions she'd made. She'd bravely thumbed her nose at anyone and everyone who tried to tell her how to live.

"She'd tell me to do whatever the hell I wanted to and not worry about what anyone else thought."

"There you go. Do whatever you want. In all the years I've known you, you've rarely made the wrong decision. You usually do the right thing."

The right thing? Misty wasn't even sure what that was.

That letter was a real pain in the ass. To open or not to open?

That was the million-dollar question.

CHAPTER THREE

"**I** read it."

Three words. Not that many but they changed everything.

When Jared had arrived at home from work, he'd found Misty and the kids in the kitchen having an after-camp snack. He'd gone into the office for part of the day but left before rush hour, anxious to get home to his family. He'd promised Misty that he'd fire up the grill and cook the chicken for dinner.

When he'd opened the door and placed his briefcase down in a chair, she'd hopped up, smiled, and given him a quick kiss. He'd wanted to linger but Lizzie and Nate would have made faces, so he instead grabbed a beer from the fridge. She'd reached around him, her hand brushing his back, for a bottle of juice to refill the kids' glasses. It was then that she'd said it. Quietly. Softly. As if she didn't want the children to hear.

"I read it."

He didn't need her to tell him what *it* was. He knew what it was. That damn letter. He should have thrown that attorney out of his office yesterday. Shit. She didn't deserve this. Her childhood had been awful enough without having to deal with a maybe-parent that had abandoned her all those years ago. His sweet Misty had made peace with her upbringing and she didn't need anyone digging into a past that was only going to upset her.

Dammit, it was *his job* to protect his wife. He'd gladly step in front of a bullet for her. That's how much she meant to him. Hadn't his father always preached to his sons about what men were supposed to do? Men were supposed to protect those that they loved and keep them from harm. This letter had come out of nowhere and Jared hadn't been prepared. Now Misty was going to get hurt again. He didn't know exactly how that was going to happen or when, but he couldn't trust Adam Reynolds to be a decent human being. If the asshole had been, he wouldn't have reached out after all this time.

He would have left well enough alone.

Because a man as wealthy as Reynolds had to have checked out Misty thoroughly before he sent that lawyer with the letter. He had to have known that she was fine, and all her needs were taken care of. She didn't need him. She had a family to take care of her now.

"We can talk about it later," he said. "When you're ready."

"I'm ready right now. Let me turn on the television for the kids."

It must be serious if she was willing to place Lizzie and Nate in front of the TV on a weekday afternoon. She liked for them to get outside if the weather cooperated, and if it didn't, she tried to get them involved in a creative activity. Today, however, she turned on cartoons, much to their delight.

She settled into a kitchen chair where they could both see the kids from where they were sitting.

"I thought you threw it away. I thought you didn't want to read it."

Jared should have let her talk, but this entire situation had taken him by surprise.

"I didn't at first," she replied, her gaze darting to the living room where Lizzie and Nate were engrossed. "But I talked to Rayne—"

"She told you to read it?"

He liked Rayne, he really did, but he wasn't happy if her best friend was pushing her to do things she didn't want to do.

"No," Misty sighed with a shake of her head. "She simply pointed out that sometime in the future I might want to read it and that perhaps throwing it away wasn't the wisest course of action. Honestly, I was already regretting it. After I hung up with her, I went upstairs and got the letter from the trash and stuck it in my sweater drawer, all the way at the bottom. For someday. If I wanted to read it."

What in the hell had happened today then?

"I guess that someday was today."

"It was," she agreed, her chin resting in her hands. She was chewing on her lower lip, her gaze far away. "It stayed in that drawer for about an hour."

A whole hour?

"Then just as Rayne predicted my curiosity got the better of me. I might not need a father in my life, but I couldn't shake the question of what he had to say. How could he possibly rationalize not coming forward until now?" She reached into her pocket and pulled out the envelope, pushing it across the table to Jared. "Turns out he didn't even try. It was a complete *mea culpa*. He says that he's a terrible, awful man that has many regrets in his life and how he's dealt with me is one of his greatest."

Jared's stomach twisted in his abdomen, bile rising in his throat. The nerve of that asshole to reach out to Misty. She had a loving and forgiving heart. Was she thinking of forgiving this bastard? He didn't deserve it.

"He's an–"

"He's dying, Jared."

Dying. The ultimate trump card.

"And you believe him?"

"Why would he lie about it?"

"Because he's lied to you your entire life? Because he wants you to forgive him or whatever he's asking for in that letter? You can't fucking argue with a dead man, right?"

Misty's brows rose and she sat straighter in the chair. "You're really fired up about this. It's only a letter."

"It's more than that," he replied, frustration in his tone. Didn't she see that Reynolds was manipulating her? "I won't let him hurt you, Misty. I won't let him."

Her expression immediately softened. "I doubt that he can. He's a stranger to me, Jared. A complete and total stranger."

"I checked him out, Mist. This guy is human garbage. He's the asshole that other assholes aspire to be. He plays dirty to win. He doesn't care who he hurts."

"He says that in the letter so I would imagine that you're right."

"He's going to play on your sympathies."

"Probably."

"You can't let him."

"Okay."

"You don't seem to understand what I'm saying."

"I do understand. But what you're not understanding is that it's in my control how I react to this. He's not in control here. I am."

Misty was always so calm. Until she wasn't. He'd been on the receiving end of more than a few of her blowups. Deservedly so. He wasn't an easy man to live with. Luckily, they were few and far between but when she was done...she was *done*.

She slid the letter closer to Jared.

"I don't have anything to hide. You can read what he said for yourself."

Jared didn't want to read what Reynolds had written. He wanted everything to go back to the way it was before yesterday. When Misty was happy, and she didn't have any painful memories dredged up by some asshole who had been missing her entire life.

He read the letter, of course. Because he certainly couldn't tell his wife that he wasn't interested or that he wasn't pissed off. She knew him well enough to know all of that already. He didn't have to say it out loud.

The letter started out with a greeting from Adam Reynolds and an explanation of who he was. Then to the heart of the matter...

You're probably wondering why I'm writing to you.

I believe that I am your father.

Reynolds hadn't pussyfooted around. He'd come right to the point.

I met your mother when she was visiting her friend Zelda in Denver.

Misty had never mentioned a family friend named Zelda but that didn't mean that she didn't exist.

We became close and I visited several times over the next several months.

Was "close" a euphemism for "sex" or something else?

One day I showed up at the cafe that your mother and Zelda frequented. I wanted to surprise her. Annette was obviously pregnant. She was definitely showing. Like the coward that I am, I backed away before she could see me and left. I didn't want to face up to the responsibility.

A complete and total asshat. Reynolds might run a billion-dollar corporation, but he had the morals of an alley cat. He'd left Misty and her mother to flounder in poverty. That alone made him a son of a bitch.

I'm dying and now face my day of reckoning. I know that I've done many things wrong. Terrible things. I don't know if I can make anything right at this late stage, but I'd like to try. I'd love to meet you and let you call me any name that you deem appropriate. It's the least that I can do. Selfishly, I'd also like to talk with you, Misty. You appear to have turned out to be a fine woman. Annette did a good job.

With no help from you, asshole. Too little, too late.

There was more but it wasn't anything earth shattering. Reynolds wanted Misty to visit him in his family home in northern California. Totally at her convenience. He apologized again and begged for contact, saying that he only wanted to make amends. He'd understand if she didn't reach out.

Jared looked up from the letter, folding it and sliding it back across to his wife. She had that look on her face that he'd seen before. They were going to have a disagreement. He might end up sleeping on the couch. Then they'd make up and compromise if they could. If they couldn't, one of them was destined to be disappointed.

I think it's going to be me.

"You're not seriously contemplating replying to this letter, are you?"

Shit, I didn't mean to start out like that. I should have eased into it. Too late now.

Misty's chin firmed and he knew immediately that he was fucked.

"I don't particularly enjoy being spoken to like that, Jared. Do you want to try again? Maybe this time you can act like I'm an adult and not Lizzie or Nate."

Sighing, he searched for the words that would make this all okay, but dammit, he wasn't that eloquent.

Or bright, apparently, if his wife's expression was to be believed. She'd crossed her arms over her chest waiting for him to say something.

"What I meant was–"

"Yes, what did you mean?" Misty broke in, her eyes narrowing dangerously. "Because you sound as if there would only be one possible outcome to this situation. Yours. We've been down this road before and it looks like we're going to do it. Again."

She spoke the truth. He had a tendency to see things in black and white, assuming that he was always right. In the beginning they'd had a few arguments over this issue and he'd become much better about it. But every now and then, old habits reared their ugly head.

"You're right," he admitted. "I am seeing this from my own perspective, but I swear I'm trying to put myself into your shoes. I honestly cannot fathom how you would think to give this waste of skin five minutes of your time after what he did to you. He left you, Misty. He ran scared. That's not what a man does."

She smiled slightly and sighed. "That's certainly not what you did. You stepped forward when I got pregnant."

"It was the best decision I've ever made in my life."

He didn't say it to kiss up. He said it because it was the truth. He couldn't imagine his life without Misty in it. He loved her and walking away from her and their baby had never crossed his mind.

"But that's not what he did," she went on. "I'm glad that you didn't run but he didn't make the same decision. I'm guessing he didn't have a Gerald Monroe helping him to become a man like you did."

From what Jared had been able to find out about the Reynolds family, Adam's father had been just as selfish and ruthless as his son.

"He doesn't deserve anything from you."

"You're right. He doesn't. But let's talk about what I deserve."

"You deserve everything."

Misty laughed at this, reaching across to place her hands on his. Her skin was warm, and he tangled their fingers together.

"I don't know about having everything. Where would we put it all?" she teased him. "Seriously, let me explain to you why I'm thinking about this and I hope you can understand."

"I'm listening."

She cocked her head and smiled again. "I know and that's what I love about you."

"That's it? My listening skills? You don't love my manly physique? Or my sense of humor?"

Rolling her eyes, she shook her head. "Definitely not your cornball sense of humor. Now shut up and listen to me. The kids won't stay quiet forever, you know."

No, they wouldn't. They'd be demanding dinner soon.

"First of all, if I decided to contact him – and I haven't decided that yet – it would be because of my needs, not his. Second, I think there's still an open question as to whether he's even my father. My mother said she wasn't sure who my father was, and I have no reason to disbelieve her. Knowing her, she might well have been with more than one man during that period, especially if Adam wasn't around all the time. She was all about grabbing at life and living it to the fullest. If he walked away, Jared, it may have been from someone else's child."

"He didn't know that, though. He's not a good person on a technicality."

"True," she conceded. "I don't have any preconceived notions that our reunion will be filled with rainbows and ponies. I have hard questions that he may not want to answer, but I also have easier ones about my mother. He knew her before I was born, and I'd like to know more about her during that time."

"After you get the answers, give him a swift kick in the ass."

"I might do that," she laughed. "From what I've read about him online today, he richly deserves it."

"He's a total jerk," Jared agreed. "He doesn't pay people well, and he treats them badly. He's not terribly well-liked by anyone."

Misty rubbed at her chin. "I guess I'm just curious. When I was younger, I wondered about my father and now I'm being given a chance to actually talk to him."

"Have you thought about him lately?"

"No, but that doesn't mean that I'm not curious. I'm not looking to establish any sort of relationship with him. I think I just want to talk to him. Maybe. I need to think about it. It's a big step."

"Take all the time you need. You know that I'll support any decision that you make."

Her brows rose. "Are you sure? I can tell that you don't want me to reply."

He shook his head. "What I don't want is for you to get hurt. That's all. I just want to protect him from being a jerk to you again."

She squeezed his hands. "You can't protect me from everything. That isn't practical. It's sweet, but not a realistic goal."

"It isn't going to stop me from trying."

"I never thought it would."

She knows me well.

"So what happens now? You just…think on this? You'll let me know sometime in the future?"

"It won't be too long. He says he's dying and trying to get his affairs in order. I would imagine that I need to make the decision sooner rather than later."

Jared tapped on the letter sitting between them on the table. "Don't let your loving and forgiving heart let you feel sorry for this guy. He's earned his spot in hell."

That statement seemed to amuse Misty because she laughed, her hand over her mouth to muffle the sound. "What makes you think I'm so loving and forgiving? I can be a real bitch sometimes."

Jared shrugged. "You forgive me all the time."

"That's because I love you."

"I love you too, baby. More than you can ever know."

He'd do anything to make sure that no one hurt her. Especially not Adam Reynolds. That guy was going to find out that redemption was something that all the money in the world couldn't buy.

CHAPTER FOUR

Later that night, Misty was soaking in a hot bath. The kids were asleep, Jared was downstairs in his home office tapping away at his laptop, and she was relaxing back, her head propped up with a bath pillow while her skin turned prune-like. She savored the silence, enjoying the peace and quiet that came so rarely in the household. She wouldn't trade her life for anything in the world, but a few more moments like this would be nice.

"Can I wash your back?"

She didn't have to open her eyes. She could feel her husband's presence in the room.

"Does that offer come with strings attached?"

"Definitely."

Giggling, she opened her eyes to Jared standing above her, a wicked grin on his gorgeous face. He was in a playful mood, and she wouldn't mind playing right back. It might get her head into a better space.

It certainly would be pleasurable. Jared would see to that.

He was waiting for an invitation, his fingers hovering at the hem of his t-shirt. He could rip it off immediately and then tear off his pants. All she had to do was say the word.

"I guess you could join me."

Maybe it was his time in the military, or maybe he was simply gifted in certain respects, but Jared Monroe could strip off his clothes faster than the speed of light. He was basically a blur for a few seconds and then he was bare-assed naked, climbing into the bathtub.

It was plenty big enough for two.

They'd wanted a large tub when they were looking for houses and this beautiful bathroom had been one of the major selling points of the home. They'd put it to good use many times.

Water sloshed against the sides as his large body sunk into the water. He'd positioned himself so that he was lying on the opposite end, her feet propped on his muscular thighs. He lifted one up and began to massage her instep with his strong fingers, dragging a groan of pure heaven from her lips.

"That feels amazing. Don't ever stop."

"I'll have to stop eventually."

"No, don't stop."

Jared chuckled, his fingertips digging into an especially sensitive spot on her heel that had her almost coming out of the water. "Only Stevie thinks everything is going to be forever."

Stevie did think that. When they left, she thought they were going to be gone forever. When they petted her, she thought it would be forever. She always looked so disgruntled when Misty would have to go back to what she was doing and take a break from petting her or scratching her belly.

"A girl can dream."

"Can't argue with a dream."

He moved to the other foot and did the same magic, rotating the ankle and then sliding his hands up her calf to massage the muscles there. Her arousal had already begun to build, and she moved restlessly under his ministrations.

"This is why I married you."

"You married me because I give foot rubs? Good to know. Want to know why I married you?"

"I already know."

"You do?"

"Of course. You have no secrets from me."

"It does make life easier."

Eventually his hands drifted farther up to her thighs and he pulled her closer until she was sitting astride him, her hands planted on his wide chest to keep her balance. And because she really liked touching him.

Leaning down, she brushed his lips with hers and his palm came up behind her head, holding there so he could deepen the kiss. Their tongues played tag as hands explored one another, gliding up and down. Her skin tingled and burned everywhere he touched and she squirmed on his already hard cock, letting him know of her impatience.

His fingers tickled her ribcage and his lips nibbled at her ear, building her urgency even more. Her entire body buzzed with pleasure and her heart beat madly, drowning out any other sounds but their sighs and moans.

His large palms cupped her breasts, the thumbs stroking the pebbled nipples until she thought she might scream but she didn't want to wake Lizzie and Nate.

"Now, Jared."

This time he wouldn't argue with her. He often liked to play and tease, extending their lovemaking as long as possible, but one look at his expression told her that this wouldn't be one of those nights. His jaw was tight and his pupils blown wide. He was as aroused – or more – than she was.

Raising herself up on her knees, she then sunk down on his

cock inch by delicious inch. This was the part where she liked taking her time, feeling all of him rub those deep, secret spots that drove her out of her mind. When she was fully seated, she paused to savor the moment, although his hands were at her hips urging her to move.

She began to sway her hips slightly, then circling them before rising up and down. Slow at first to build the tempo, and then faster as the pleasure built, pushing her to the edge of the precipice. White hot heat poured through her veins as they found the perfect tempo, pushing both of them higher into the stars. She was so close...

His thumb found her clit and that was all it took. She burst into a million pieces, white lights flashing behind her lids. Jared's body bowed and his fingers tightened on her bottom as his own climax sent him over the edge. Eventually, she collapsed on top of him, resting her head on his chest where she could hear his galloping heart.

They didn't move for a long time, content to be close. They whispered softly about the weather for tomorrow and the next television show they wanted to binge. When the water cooled, they had to reluctantly climb out of the tub. Jared dried her off and then himself while she slipped into a pair of pajama shorts and a t-shirt.

They tossed their towels in the hamper, brushed their teeth, and then slid into bed to watch some television. Misty snuggled next to Jared, but her mind was far away from the two of them. She'd been thinking about it and she'd made a decision.

To be honest, she'd made the decision before she was even in the bathtub. He might not be happy about it, but she couldn't deny the need in her heart.

"I want to meet Adam Reynolds."

Jared didn't respond right away so she looked up at him,

trying to figure out what he was thinking by the expression on his face. To her surprise he just looked normal, as if she'd mentioned wanting to take a trip to the grocery store.

"I had a feeling that you were going to say that. I'll talk to Jason and Logan about taking a long weekend."

"Are you mad?"

He shook his head, his smile gentle. "No, baby, I'm not mad. I'm not thrilled with Adam Reynolds but it's only natural that you'd want to meet him. I get that, and I actually agree. You can meet him and talk to him. Then decide for yourself what you want to do from there."

She was going to meet her maybe father, and she wasn't sure how she felt about it all.

She only knew that if she didn't take this chance, she'd regret it.

Okay, let's do this. Let's meet Adam Reynolds.

CHAPTER FIVE

Jared drove the car through the imposing iron gates and down the long driveway toward the home of Adam Reynolds. From the gate neither he nor Misty could see the house, and it took a few minutes of driving before a section peeked out from behind the large trees lining either side of the road.

The trees were lush with green leaves at this time of the year. With the car windows down he could smell the rain that had only stopped falling a few miles ago, making everything around them fresh and new.

The grounds of the Reynolds estate were beautiful with plentiful trees and thick green grass that would have made Pebble Beach cry with envy. The large house was set far back from the road for optimum privacy and there wasn't a neighbor for miles. The home itself could only be described as a mansion, built in stone with an impressive entryway with six pillars guarding the front door. Above the entrance was Adam Reynolds' monogram.

In gold letters.

"I can see he doesn't have a problem with conspicuous consumption," Jared said, his gaze taking in the luxurious surroundings. "I'm waiting for a butler in tie and tails to tell me that Lady Mary is expecting us for tea in the east drawing room."

Laughing, Misty pushed open her door. "We'll never know until we ring the doorbell. Are you ready?"

Was he ready? He wasn't entirely sure. Was she? She'd been fairly quiet for most of the drive.

This had all happened so quickly he'd barely had a chance to process it. After Misty had decided to reply to her possible father's letter, she'd called the attorney back the next day. Within twenty-four hours they'd made arrangements for the kids to stay with Reed and Kaylee and for Jared and Misty to travel down to northern California to meet Adam Reynolds.

Lizzie and Nate were thrilled because they were going to get spoiled beyond belief with Uncle Reed and Aunt Kaylee. The dog and cat were even more happy because they got to hang out with Reed and Kaylee's Golden Retriever named Isabella.

Misty was excited because she might be meeting the man that was her father, plus they were getting away for a few days – just the two of them. They hadn't done that in over a year.

Jared? He wasn't as happy as everyone else. He still wasn't sure this was a good idea, but he was open to being convinced. Hopefully, Reynolds wouldn't be as much of a jerk as he was purported to be.

I'm the eternal optimist.

Now two weeks later they were ringing the doorbell of a man that might be his wife's father. Maybe. He wasn't convinced yet.

"Just remember, babe, if at any point you want to leave just say the word."

They'd already chosen a "safe word" of sorts – *umbrella.* Misty would ask Jared if he'd remembered to bring their umbrella. If she said that, he'd hustle her out the door without a backward glance to their host. Fuck Reynolds. The only person that mattered here was Misty.

"Let's hope it doesn't come to that."

He hoped that as well, although he couldn't shake a nasty case of foreboding about this entire trip to meet Adam Reynolds. He doubted anything good was going to come from this, but he really, honestly wanted to be wrong. He wanted Misty to get whatever closure she needed, and her questions answered.

Although if it had been Jared, he would have told the billionaire to pound sand.

None of the research he'd done in the last two weeks made him feel any better about this meeting. Few people had anything nice to say about Reynolds. He was well-respected by other shark businessmen, but regular folks weren't as kind. His own sister didn't speak to him.

"You can still change your mind. We can make a run for the car."

"They'd probably know. I'm guessing they have a lot of security."

At the very least there had been a camera at the entrance. The gates to the estate had opened for him without him having to even pick up a phone or send a text. He ran his gaze around the immediate area, but he didn't see any other cameras. They had to be there, though. A billionaire couldn't be too careful. He was actually surprised there wasn't a guard at the gate. Anyone could have climbed it if they were determined enough.

Jared rang the bell and waited, placing his arm around Misty's shoulders. He wanted her to know he was here for her. This had to be an extremely emotional meeting and his wife had such a soft heart.

The door opened and a middle-aged woman in a gray dress stood on the other side. She wasn't smiling in welcome, but she hadn't slammed the door in their faces either.

"You must be the Monroes." She stepped back so they could enter. "We've been expecting you."

We?

Reynolds was divorced and his children were all old enough to have their own homes, but this place was large enough to house several families and they wouldn't have to see each other very often. Unless they wanted to. Jared loved his siblings, but he was damn happy that he didn't live in the same house as his sister Becky. She was best experienced in small doses.

The foyer of the home was just as impressive as the outside, with marble floors and soaring ceilings. A sweeping staircase that belonged in an old Hollywood film was to their left, complete with a dark mahogany railing and crimson carpeting that led to the landing on the upper floor.

A pretty young woman with long dark hair stood up there looking down on them. She wasn't very old, perhaps late teens or early twenties. She didn't say anything, just stared for a few seconds and then turned and walked away, disappearing down a hallway.

"That was Taylor," the woman said. "Adam's granddaughter. I'm sorry she didn't greet you. She can get moody at times but then that's the norm with young people, isn't it? Follow me and I'll take you to Adam."

The woman, who hadn't introduced herself, led them into a hallway under the staircase all the way to a door at the end. She knocked briefly but didn't wait for anyone to speak, pushing the heavy wooden door open so they could enter.

"Adam, the Monroes are here."

Jared had seen photos of Adam Reynolds when he'd re-searched the billionaire, so his appearance wasn't a surprise. He'd shown Misty some pictures as well, but she was currently gazing at him as if trying to imprint every detail of his features indelibly into her brain.

She was looking for a resemblance between them.

Frankly, he didn't see any. Reynolds had been blond in his youth and he had blue eyes as well, but that was the end of it as far as Jared could tell. Their noses, brows, hairline, even lips were different. It didn't mean that he wasn't her father, though. He'd seen pictures of Misty's mother and she definitely favored that side of the family.

Reynolds rounded the side of his large desk, a wide smile on his face. His hair was graying, the front slightly receding but that seemed to be the only concession to age. Despite his declaration of being at death's door he looked fit, trim, and tanned.

"Misty, welcome to my home," he said warmly, holding his arms out as if he was going to try to hug her. Jared stiffened instinctively, not wanting his wife to be put on the spot. Reynolds, however, didn't go for any more contact than a two-handed handshake. "My god, you look just like your mother. The spitting image. She was so incredibly beautiful. Inside and out."

And yet you left her pregnant and poor. Asshole.

The billionaire swung his attention to Jared, finally letting go of Misty's hands.

"And you are Jared Monroe. Your reputation precedes you. I read about your part in the apprehension of Wade Bryson."

Jared fucking hated it when people brought up that homicidal bastard. Besides, he hadn't really done all that much. Logan had done the heavy lifting in that case.

He shook hands with the older man anyway, not wanting to appear churlish, but it probably didn't matter. Adam Reynolds' complete attention was back on Misty.

"It's just so eerie looking at you. You look so much like her."

Reynolds chuckled and ran his fingers through his short hair. "I'm sorry to keep going on about it. She named you Misty after her favorite book, didn't she? *Misty of Chincoteague.*"

Misty's brows rose. "She told you about that?"

"We talked about so many things."

They'd done more than talk if Misty was any evidence.

"Please, forgive my poor manners," the older man apologized. "Please have a seat. Can I get you anything to drink or eat? I can just ring up the kitchen staff and you can have anything that you want."

Misty and Jared settled into a leather couch while Reynolds sat in a brown leather chair. The library was impressive with walls covered in books and a fireplace nestled in the corner, unlit at this time of year. Over the mantle was a large painting of two children who Jared assumed belonged to Reynolds. He had a son and a daughter.

Jared glanced at Misty, but she shook her head. "We're fine, thank you."

Reynolds appeared to be nervous, rubbing his hands together, his feet dancing even though he was seated. "I've so been looking forward to you visiting. I've talked about nothing else to Lydia."

"Lydia?" Misty asked. "Is she your daughter?"

"No, she's my…significant other, I guess you could say. She's the one that answered the door. I'm divorced and Lydia was once my assistant. Now she runs the house. And my life, but she does a much better job than I ever could. My daughter's name is Dahlia and my son David."

"We saw your granddaughter at the top of the stairs," Misty said. "She's lovely."

The older man's smile widened. Clearly, he was fond of his granddaughter. "I'm very proud of Taylor. She's smart as a whip.

She's going to Stanford in the fall. She wants to be a doctor, she says."

His smile wavered and then his shoulders slumped. "She says that she wants to research a cure for cancer. She's always been a wonderful child. I don't deserve her."

At this point, Jared was of the opinion that Adam Reynolds didn't deserve Misty either, but he'd love to be proven wrong.

"We don't have to talk about it if you don't want to," Mistry replied softly, her expression softening. "It's personal, after all."

Except that it was the entire reason that they were sitting in this room, talking to this man.

Reynolds shook his head. "No, it's fine. I've accepted my fate. I went through all the stages, including bargaining, but even with all my money I can't outrun death. I have late stage pancreatic cancer and there isn't much they can do. They wanted me to get treatment to extend my life a few months, but I don't want to be sick at the end. I want to enjoy the time I have left. They say I'll probably be gone before Christmas. That's why I had to contact you, Misty. I have to try and put right all the bad things I've done in my life."

"That's why I'm here," she murmured, her gaze dropping to her handbag where her fingers were pleating the leather strap. "I want to hear your story."

"You're a good person to listen. Not many people would."

"That's true," Jared said, his tone hard. "Misty has always had a soft heart and I wouldn't want anyone to take advantage of that."

He could almost *hear* his wife rolling her eyes at his protective statement, but he didn't care. He wasn't going to let some asshole walk all over his wife.

Reynolds nodded. "I understand what you're saying, of course. I know you don't trust me and, frankly, I haven't given you any reason to. I just want a chance to put my life into order before I go."

"You're not even sure that Misty is your daughter," Jared reminded him. "So there may not be anything to fix."

"Say the word and I can have a doctor in here for a cheek swab in less than an hour. But I do believe that I'm your father, Misty." Reynolds placed a hand on his chest. "I know it in here."

Straightening in her chair, Misty glanced over at Jared. "Then I have some questions."

"I'll answer them all."

This was Jared's cue to leave them on their own. He and his wife had discussed this, and she was adamant that she have some time alone with Adam Reynolds to talk about her mother. Although Jared had heard many stories about Misty's mother, he had a feeling there were a few that had been held back. For good reason, if the stories he'd heard were true. She'd had a tumultuous upbringing to say the least.

Jared stood and then bent down to drop a kiss on Misty's forehead. "If you don't mind, I think I'll go and check out the house and grounds while you two chat."

He might be giving them time alone, but he still didn't trust Adam Reynolds. That made him one of two things...

A cynical asshole or right. Only time would tell which.

CHAPTER SIX

Misty could certainly see why her mother had become involved with Adam Reynolds. Even with an advanced stage cancer, he was a handsome man. She'd seen photos of him, of course, when she'd done some research, but nothing had prepared her for the sheer charisma the older man exuded. She had to wonder if he'd always been that way or had his success given him extreme self-confidence?

Annette Foster had loved a swaggering bad boy; at least that's what she'd told her daughter. Misty hadn't understood when she was a child, but later she had understood all too well, vowing that she'd never end up with a man like that. She'd kept her word too, marrying Jared who could never have carried a label like that. He was far too ethical and upstanding, although he could be the very devil in the bedroom.

But that was a different topic altogether.

"You don't look sick," she blurted when Jared left the room. "I mean…I'm sorry, but you look really healthy."

"The irony of pancreatic cancer," he replied with a tight smile. "I don't look like I'm dying but I can assure you that I am. You can talk to my doctor if you like. I don't want to keep any secrets from you, Misty."

"I believe you," she assured him, fidgeting in her chair slightly. This wasn't the easiest of conversations and her heart was beating a mile a minute. Her palms were even a little sweaty, but she didn't want to wipe them down her jeans in front of him. "So can you tell me about my mother? I mean…about your relationship?"

Sitting back, a smile played around his mouth. "The day I met your mother will always be clear in my memory. It was a Friday and I was spending the weekend in Denver visiting a friend from college. Your mother and her girlfriend Zelda were sitting a few tables away at a cafe. I could hear her laughter and that made me turn and look at her. She was so beautiful and full of life. I just had to meet her. So I had the waitress give me their bill. When they found out I'd paid for their dinner, they came over to say thank you. That's when I asked your mother out on a date. I was young and brash back then, full of confidence. It never occurred to me that she would turn me down."

"Did she? Turn you down?"

"She said yes."

That sounded like Annette Foster. Her zest for living was legendary and if a handsome man had bought her dinner and asked her out, she would have said yes. She'd always been the adventurous type, grabbing onto life with both hands and holding on for the ride. Misty, on the other hand, would have been instantly suspicious. She hadn't taken after her mother in that way.

For so many reasons, but mostly because the people of Fielding, Montana hadn't taken kindly to Annette's sense of adventure. She simply hadn't fit in with the townsfolk's idea of what a single mother should be and they'd persecuted her – and Misty – for not fitting in. Annette hadn't cared much about being accepted but her daughter had.

"I took her out the next day," Adam went on. "We spent the whole day together driving around and seeing the sights. She was so much fun and she made me laugh. I loved her spontaneity. My childhood had been rather regimented, and she was a breath of fresh air."

"You were already married?"

Clearing his throat, Adam nodded. "Yes, I was already married to Sandra. I'm not proud of my actions. Your mother said she wasn't looking for any commitment. She just wanted to have fun. Her friend was like that too, always laughing and having a good time."

"I remember mom talking about her friend Zelda, but I never met her. She sent me birthday presents for several years."

Then the gifts had stopped. Misty didn't know why but she assumed now that her mother and Zelda had some sort of falling out or simply drifted apart.

"Zelda wasn't her real name, you know. It was a nickname that she'd earned because she liked to go out and party. Her actual name was Amelia Banks. She passed away when you were just a child. Car accident. Very tragic."

That explained why the gifts had stopped. It also might be an explanation as to why Annette's "party" behavior had escalated at that point, the nights becoming longer and the drinking more plentiful.

"I didn't know that. That's very sad. Mom never mentioned it to me." Misty shrugged awkwardly. "I assume she knew."

"She probably did. She was close to Zelda's brother and sister. They would have told her."

There was a pause in the conversation, the tension growing. Misty could feel his reluctance to continue but this was what she was here for. To hear his story. She waited patiently while he collected his thoughts, not prodding him or trying to put words in his mouth.

"We grew close," he finally said, his gaze somewhere far off. He was remembering and she wished she could see those images of her mother young and carefree. Misty's own memories were dominated by the time at the end when Annette was sick and dying. "I'd like to tell you that I fell in love with Annette, but I doubt that I was even capable of the emotion back then. I was young and selfish, and I only thought about myself. Hell, that's pretty much what I've done my whole life, to be honest. I was a taker and I took from your mother. I enjoyed my time with her, but I never intended it to be anything more. I visited my friend when Annette said she'd be there with Zelda. We had fun. Your mother had the ability to make a person feel special."

That was a facet of her mother's personality that she hadn't seen but she didn't discount Adam's statement. Annette might have been quite different before her daughter was born.

"And then she got pregnant," Misty said, watching his expression closely. "So you left."

"I haven't been a good person," he explained with a grimace. "As a matter of fact, I've been a real son of a bitch, thinking only of myself. I'm sure you already know that about me, though. I checked you and your husband Jared out before sending that letter and from what I found out I have no doubt whatsoever that *he* checked *me* out too. His reputation as a lawman precedes him."

"He doesn't want to talk about Wade Bryson," Misty replied quickly. "Don't bring it up."

"I won't," Adam promised. "I also learned about his family."

"They're wonderful people. Some of the best I've ever known."

She wasn't just saying that. It was the truth.

"I'm glad that you had them. I'm only sorry that I wasn't a better man for you. If it's any consolation I was a lousy father to my other children. They pretty much hate me, and I don't blame them."

"I'm sure they don't hate you."

"Maybe. They might just feel nothing for me. I wasn't there for them, either. My ex-wife Sandra says that I lack empathy. She's probably right. She usually is. At least that's what she told me when we were married," he chuckled.

He didn't seem all that bothered by the fact that his own children might hate him. Misty would be devastated if Lizzie and Nate hated her.

"So my mother got pregnant," Misty prompted. "And you left."

Adam's smile dimmed. "I did and I'm not proud of that. As I said I was young and selfish. My only defense is that I would have been a lousy father. I wasn't cut out to be a parent, if I'm honest."

"And married."

"That too."

If Misty were going to be honest right back, she would have said that Annette Foster wasn't cut out for parenthood either. But she wouldn't say that. Her mother had done her best, but her idea of motherhood was unusual. She had managed to give Misty a spine of steel and the determination to make something of herself despite all the naysayers.

"I'm almost forty now. You've waited a long time for a reunion."

"And I would have waited longer," Adam said sadly, "if I hadn't become ill. Facing your mortality makes you examine your life closely. It makes you see yourself in ways you never would have before. I now see that I've made so many mistakes. I can't hope to right them all but I'm hoping that I can with you, Misty."

Those were pretty words...

"Why should I believe you after all of this time? Why should I even care? I've done pretty well without you."

"You've done just fine without me—"

"I know."

On one hand she wanted to get to know this man, but on the other she wasn't feeling all that charitable. Her childhood had pretty much sucked. She didn't think about it much anymore, didn't dwell on it, but he'd brought all this stuff up again after she'd thought she'd laid it to rest. Now she had to deal with it. Again.

He was going to have to do that, too. It was only fair.

"But you're here," he went on. "That must mean that you are at least curious."

"I am, but I'm not sure what you want from me. Forgiveness? Absolution? I'm not sure that I can give you any of that. And even if I could, I'm not sure that I want to."

"I'm not asking for forgiveness," he said quickly with a shake of his head. "I know I'm far too late for that. My hope is that I can somehow make it up to you. At the very least answer your questions about your father. You must have had many as you grew up. Then of course, to allow you to yell at me. Call me names. It's your right to do that and I won't deny you the opportunity."

Misty didn't want to call him names or scream and yell. She didn't want to call anyone names, although there were moments when she was driving and someone would pull out in front of her that she was quite tempted.

At this point, she didn't feel enough for Adam Reynolds to conjure up that much emotion for him, positive or negative.

Perhaps if they got to know one another she might eventually become angry.

Especially if she liked him. She wasn't sure how she felt about him at the present time.

"Actually, what I really want is to ask you a question. All these years…did you ever think about me and Mom? Did you ever feel any regrets or guilt?"

She already knew the answer. His expression gave it away. To his credit, he wasn't trying to hide it.

"Not really, no. I don't think I can emphasize enough, Misty, just how much of a jerk I've been my whole life. Until recently, I didn't care about anyone else but myself. You deserve the truth and I won't lie to make myself look better. If I thought about your mom at any point, I pushed it out of my mind completely. I wouldn't allow myself to have regrets or guilt because those emotions would get in the way of my goals. I didn't have time for sentimentality. Love and friendship were alien concepts to me. I only knew competition, winning, and losing. That's it."

Full marks for honesty, but it painted a tragic portrait of a man who had wasted his life in pursuit of success. He wouldn't die alone because he had the money to make sure that someone was with him. Who that someone was, however, might simply be a paid employee, not family. According to him, his own children didn't like him.

Did she like him?

She didn't know him well enough to like or hate him. At the present, she didn't feel anything for him except sadness. So much wasted. He could have done so much with his life, but he didn't. But he'd made his choices and now he would have to lie – and die – with them.

"I appreciate your honesty," she finally said after he finished. "It would probably have been easier to lie to me and tell me you thought about me every day. But of course that wouldn't be true. I didn't think about you, either. You don't miss what you've never had."

"If I could go back in time… Let's just say that I'd do a lot of things differently."

"So contacting me isn't to make you feel better? It's only to make me feel better? Or is it a bid to save your soul?"

"You're a smart one," he chuckled, rubbing his chin. "I would have loved for you to work in my stores. I think you would have made excellent decisions. As for my soul? I know which direction I'm headed, and it isn't into a warm light. I've been told that I'll burn in hell for the things I've done, and I think that they're probably right. Anything I do now would just be a drop in the bucket. There's no way to balance the scales even if I lived to be a hundred."

"So why bother?"

"I've come to the realization, rather late in life I will admit, that what I want or need isn't the most important thing."

"You might not even be my father. Mom always said she didn't know who my father was."

He tapped his chest again, as before. "I know in here that I am. How about we get a DNA test so I can prove it to you?"

Misty wasn't sure she even wanted a father at this juncture in her life. It was far too late, in her opinion. But…

Deep down, she wanted to know the truth. Was Adam Reynolds her father?

"Fine, let's do it."

It wouldn't change anything. Right?

CHAPTER SEVEN

After Jared left the study so that Reynolds and Misty could speak privately, he wandered around the house for a bit. There were more hallways and doors than he could count, and he hadn't even strayed from the first floor. He'd never located the kitchen, but he'd managed to find himself in some sort of fitness and exercise room that overlooked the backyard and pool area.

Passing through the French doors, he stepped out onto the patio and let the warmth of the sun sink into his bones. He far preferred being outside in the nice weather than stuck inside, no matter how expensive the home furnishings.

"Who are you?"

Jared whirled around at the question and saw a man, probably mid-thirties, standing there. He had his hands on his hips and his stance was slightly aggressive as if he was trying to scare Jared off. He was tall and thin with thick blond curls, wearing jeans and a button-down shirt. Was this perhaps David, the son?

"I'm Jared Monroe. My wife Misty is here visiting with Adam Reynolds."

Not that it's any of your business.

The man visibly relaxed, his shoulders dropping. "Oh. Right. Dad mentioned that you were coming."

Jared stepped forward and held out his hand. "You must be David then."

"I am." David's gaze ran around the backyard. "Where is your wife? I'd like to meet her."

That was a surprise to Jared. He'd assumed that the entire situation would be awkward and weird between Misty and any other legitimate children, if not downright hostile.

"She's in the study with your father."

"Better her than me."

Jared wasn't quite sure how to respond to that. So he didn't.

"Beautiful home," he observed, keeping the conversation neutral. "Lovely area, too. We drove through the little town and it was quite picturesque. Have you always lived here?"

"It's a prison," David said bluntly, a strange smile on his face. "An expensively designed and decorated penitentiary. Personally, I'm doing life with no hope of parole, but I do get time off for good behavior. You should run while you can. Dad likes to keep his family close so he can keep an eye on them and control their lives. By the end of the weekend, he'll have convinced both of you that you should live here. Mark my words."

Okay, that was bizarre. I knew that Reynolds wasn't a popular guy, but it appeared his own son didn't like him.

"We aren't staying the weekend," Jared replied, ignoring most of the man's words. "We only came so that Misty and your father could meet."

At that David threw his head back and laughed. "So naive. You're not going anywhere. I guarantee you that your suitcases are already upstairs in one of the suites. It's Taylor's birthday tonight and there is no way that the old bastard won't pressure you to stay for the party. Then it will of course be too late to drive to the nearest hotel which is over sixty miles away. You're stuck here, I'm afraid. Might as well get comfortable. This is going to be your new home."

Nope. Not at all. That wasn't going to happen.

Jared was more than willing and able to pack his suitcases and get the fuck out of here. If for some strange reason he couldn't do it himself – and that was unlikely – he had friends who would love to see some action and break him out of here. In fact, they'd enjoy the hell out of it. He could already imagine Logan rappelling down the side of this fancy mansion and swinging through a huge picture window, shattering glass everywhere.

"I'll take my chances. I doubt that's going to happen."

"Suit yourself." David shrugged carelessly, and then turned on his heel to walk away. "But don't say I didn't warn you."

The last part was thrown over his shoulder as Jared watch the man's retreating figure disappear into the house. Clearly, money hadn't purchased any happiness for David Reynolds. The granddaughter Taylor hadn't exactly given them a warm welcome, either. Were they all this cold and detached? Bitter?

I'll consider myself warned.

He wasn't so damn sure about staying the night here, either. He wanted Misty to get to know her probable father but so far, he hadn't been impressed with the Reynolds family. It might make more sense to leave and come back another day. He'd gladly drive her back tomorrow so she could spend more time.

To be honest? He had a bad feeling about this whole situation.

✧   ✧   ✧   ✧

"It's just a little family party," Misty said later when they were alone in the opulent suite in the east wing of the mansion. "I'd like to get to know them."

As David had predicted, their luggage had been taken from the backseat of their car and into the house. Jared didn't have any issues with carrying them back down, but his wife sounded like she wanted to stay for the party.

"We can stay if you want to stay."

Sighing, she crossed her arms over her chest. That was the sign that she was rapidly losing patience with him.

"We can stay and you can feel sorry for yourself all evening," she sighed. "What's gotten into you? We came here to spend time and get to know Adam. You said yourself that the nearest hotel was an hour away, so what's wrong with spending the night here? It doesn't commit us to anything."

He wasn't so sure of that.

"You're on a first name basis with him already?"

She threw up her arms in frustration. "What was I supposed to call him? He might be my father."

"At least you're not calling him *daddy*. You know none of his kids even like him. I talked to his son earlier and he likened this house to a prison."

Two short steps and she was right in front of him, her finger pointing into his chest.

"Bottom line it, Jared Monroe. What's really eating you? And don't say staying the night here because that's not it. Spill it, handsome or you're sleeping on one of those lounge chairs by the pool."

That was the last thing that Jared wanted to do. The days might be sunny, but the nights were chilly.

Shit. He was going to sound like a jerk.

"I think he's using you to buy his way into heaven. He wants redemption and he wants you to forgive all the shitty things he's done in his life so that he doesn't go to hell and sit at the right hand of Lucifer. Which is what he probably deserves, by the way."

"You're probably right. I did ask him that. If he was using me as way to find redemption. He swears that isn't true. He says that he knows it's too late and that he's done too many bad things."

"When someone tells you who they are, believe them. He's told you he's no good."

"And yet here I am."

Well…yes. Normally, Misty didn't trust easily.

"I just can't believe that you think that he has a decent bone in his body. He's proven time and again that he doesn't."

"I think he probably is a terrible human being."

"Then why are we here?"

Rubbing her temples, she sat down on the king-sized bed. "Jared, I'm not sure that you can truly understand this."

"Give me a shot. I can try."

"Because I grew up without a father and barely had a mother. In a few months Adam Reynolds might be gone, and this is my one chance to get to know him before he dies. That's all I want. To get to know my father a little bit. I'm not fooling myself that I'm going to get the daddy that I always wanted and dreamed about. That ship has sailed. I just want to talk to him. That's it. Nothing more. You had a family. A real one. I didn't have that, and this is as close as I'm ever going to get. I know to you it seems lousy but it's all I've got."

A lump the size of Montana had taken up residence in his throat. At moments like this, he was well aware that he didn't deserve his wife. She was far too good for him. And extremely patient.

"You have my family. They love you. I love you. Our kids

love you. Hell, even the dog likes you best. Who knows about the cat? He's a riddle but I'm guessing he likes you better as well. You feed him."

"I love your family," she replied quietly, her gaze still down. "And I love you and the family we've created. But just once, for a little while, I'd like to have a father. Just for a few days. For one night I won't be Misty, the bastard child of Annette Foster, the town floozy."

His wife had scars – deep ones that couldn't be seen with the naked eye – regarding her tumultuous upbringing. He'd tried over the years to smooth it all away, wrapping her in the love and comfort of his home and family but at times like this he knew it wasn't enough. It would never be. Wounds like this didn't ever really heal.

She'd been a scared, lonely child who was often hungry and cold. She'd been ostracized and bullied. She wasn't any of those things now but inside of her there was still a piece of that child that he couldn't wish away. He could only hope to love her more than she'd ever believed could be possible.

He would die for this woman, then come back to life, and die for her all over again. He wanted to take away all her pain and sorrow into himself so she didn't have to feel it anymore.

"Do you know how much I love you?"

His voice sounded thick and choked to his own ears. Tears burned the back of his eyes and he quickly blinked them away. His father had always told him that men don't cry but that was a big lie. Jared had cried on his wedding day. He'd cried when Lizzie and Nate were born.

She looked up then, her own eyes shiny with tears, but her lips were smiling. "I think I might. I love you too, Jared. You're the love of my life."

"If you want to stay, then that's what we'll do. I can stand a few more hours of Adam Reynolds."

Reaching up, she looped her arms around his neck and then brushed her lips over his. His heart lurched against his ribs and his stomach flipped in his abdomen. He'd never get over the way he reacted to this woman. He was like a teenager with his first crush.

"It's only one night. We'll leave tomorrow. I promise." She giggled and rubbed the tips of their noses together. "You never know. You might enjoy yourself."

There was a better than average chance that wasn't going to happen.

Bring on the Reynolds family anyway. Just how bad could a little party be?

Chapter Eight

Misty checked her appearance one more time in the bathroom mirror. They hadn't brought any fancy clothes on this trip as they hadn't expected to need them, but she had packed her favorite blue wrap dress and a pair of matching pumps. Adam had assured her that it was a casual gathering as Taylor's friends were teenagers, but Misty wanted to wear something a little more special than her favorite blue jeans.

She swiped on some lipstick and joined Jared back in the bedroom where he was slipping on his shoes.

"You look handsome."

He did all the time but the sweater he was wearing was a particular favorite of hers. The blue of the cashmere v-neck was the exact same shade as his eyes. He'd paired it with a casual pair of khaki slacks and he'd shaved his square jaw clean. Her fingers itched to reach out and caress it while giving his neck a sniff. He always smelled so good after a shower.

If she did that, however, they might never get to the party on time.

"You look pretty awesome, too. Are you ready?"

"I am." She linked her arm with his. "Thank you for doing

this."

He shook his head as they headed down to the dining room on the first floor. "This isn't a hardship, sweetheart. It's all good. I just wanted to make sure that you don't get hurt here this weekend. That's all. You made a good point. It doesn't matter whether we stay here or at a hotel."

"You're being very calm and rational this evening."

"I can get like that sometimes."

Calm and rational was Jared's usual state but he'd made it clear that he didn't trust Adam. She wasn't so sure that she did either, but she was willing to put that aside to get to know him a little.

As they descended the sweeping staircase, Misty's nerves kicked into high gear. These weren't just random people she was meeting tonight. They might be... *family*. Blood relatives. She didn't have any of those that she knew of. Her mother had been an only child. There might be a second cousin twice removed floating around out there, but if so, Misty wasn't aware.

Jared paused at the bottom of the staircase. "Are you alright? Your hand is shaking."

He was always so aware of the little things. He never ceased to amaze her.

"It just hit me that these people might be related to me. You know... in a way."

"That may not be something that you celebrate by the end of the evening. If they take after Adam Reynolds, it might be better to be alone. Besides, you don't know if he's your real father. You'd have to take a test for that."

"I did. Take the test, I mean. This afternoon when I was visiting with Adam."

Jared's brows pinched together. "You didn't mention that earlier."

"With everything that has happened today, it was kind of lost in the details. I told him that I wanted to take the test and he called the doctor. He was there within the hour, just as he said."

"Money opens a lot of doors," Jared agreed. He leaned down, concern in his expression. "Are you going to be okay if the test comes up negative?"

"I've thought about that," she assured him. "Honestly, I'll be shocked if it's positive. I'm expecting it to be negative. I think if my mom knew who my father was that she would have told me. She wasn't the type to lie. I doubt that Adam was the only man that she was seeing, especially as it was an on and off thing when they were both in Denver."

"Cheating on his wife."

"That too. I guess you could say I didn't win the parental lottery."

Misty didn't say it to make Jared feel crappy. She'd said it because it was the truth. However, it still had that effect. He looked guilty as hell.

"Don't," she said, tugging at his sleeve. "It's not your fault you had great parents and I didn't. It's the luck of the draw. I'm just determined that our kids will have a better childhood than I did."

They turned left at the bottom of the stairs and went down the hallway to one of the large living rooms. Adam had showed her around earlier so she wouldn't get lost tonight.

"There you are," Lydia said, a welcoming smile on her face. She was also dressed casually in a silky yellow dress with spaghetti straps. "I thought we might have to send out a search party. It's easy to lose your way in this house."

Lydia was standing next to two other women that Misty hadn't seen before but there was a slight resemblance between them. One about her own age, the other older, possibly late fifties or early sixties. The younger woman was wearing white slacks and an orange blouse, while the older was dressed in a white pantsuit that set off her golden tan.

"I'm playing bartender tonight until Adam joins us," Lydia said. "What's your poison?"

Misty wasn't much of a drinker having grown up around a mother who imbibed far too much and often.

"I'll just have a soft drink."

"A beer would be fine if you have it. Otherwise I'll have a soft drink as well," Jared said. "Can I give you a hand?"

"It's all covered." Lydia handed Jared a bottle of imported beer and proceeded to pour soda over ice for Misty. "You might want to order something stronger. This family can be difficult to deal with it times. By the way, I've been very remiss in not introducing you to Dahlia and Sandra."

That explained the resemblance. Adam had mentioned his ex-wife Sandra. Sandra would be Dahlia and David's mother and Taylor's grandmother. It was nice that they could get together for the sake of the children.

"It's nice to meet you," Sandra said, extending her hand. "I hope you're enjoying your visit. I believe that Adam said that you're from the Seattle area?"

"We are now. Before we lived in Montana."

"If I'd known how handsome the men in Montana were, I'd have moved there years ago," Dahlia said, her attention focused on Jared. "Do you have any brothers, by any chance?"

"Two, but I'm afraid they're otherwise engaged."

Dahlia sighed and sipped at her martini. "That's always the way. Now where is Taylor? She was supposed to be down here already. The buffet is set up in the dining room. We need to start the party."

"She's hanging out with her friends upstairs," Sandra said in a soothing tone. "She's eighteen and she wants to have fun. She doesn't want to party with a bunch of old people."

"She'll do as she's told," Dahlia replied shortly. "Lydia, go get Taylor."

Lydia didn't move at all, simply chuckling at the command. "I'm not the hired help, dear. Go find her yourself."

Whoa. There's some tension here.

"Dahlia, don't be tiresome," Sandra said, then turned her attention back to Misty and Jared. "I do apologize. We're a family but we have our moments. Do you have children?"

They all discussed having kids for a little while until Adam came to join them. A few minutes later Taylor and about a half dozen other teenagers entered the room loudly with a lot of laughter and stomping. Unlike earlier today, Taylor was smiling and giggling, her arm linked with that of a handsome young man.

"That's Brent," Sandra said, leaning down to whisper in Misty's ear. "They've been dating for about a year. He adores her. They're going to the same university in the fall. They're the cutest couple. He's an excellent student as well. Very intelligent. He'll make a good husband."

He did appear to adore Taylor, his gaze rarely straying away from the dark-haired beauty. In Misty's opinion, however, it might be too soon to have them married off. Eighteen was young and they both had a great deal of growing up to do still.

At some point Taylor had changed clothes and she was wearing a cute little skirt with a white blouse and a bolero jacket. Most of the other teenagers were in ripped skinny jeans and sweaters.

"They look cute together."

The other teenagers were all talking and laughing. There was another couple as well among the young people – a pretty girl with long dark hair much like Taylor's.

"That's Cara and her boyfriend Lane," Sandra explained. "And those girls over there are Mandy, Emma, and Jasmine. They all go to school together."

Misty felt about a hundred years old compared to these teenagers who clearly didn't want to be with the adults this evening. They were pointedly ignoring anyone over the age of eighteen. Which was...everyone.

Two men about Misty's age strode in, one in casual clothing and the other in a business suit. The former looked a great deal like Dahlia and a little like Adam so she assumed he must be David. Jared had told her about their encounter in the backyard.

"Dad," David called out. "Tom is here for you to sign some papers."

Ah, Tom. Adam had mentioned him as well. He was Adam's personal assistant and right-hand man at Chipper Shopper.

Adam grimaced. "Duty calls. Why don't you all go ahead into the dining room and get some food? I'll join you in a few minutes."

"Ask Tom to join us as well," Lydia said, handing Adam a fresh drink. "He's practically family."

David already had a drink in his hand. He also reeked of whisky, his nose red and his eyes glassy. "And you know how we treat family around here."

"Shut up, David," Sandra said under her breath. "Can't we have one nice evening?"

David took another gulp of his drink. "Apparently not, Mother."

Jared may have made a valid point. Being a part of this family might not be a positive thing. They didn't seem to like one another very much. The friendliest so far were Adam's ex-wife and his current girlfriend. The two people one wouldn't expect to get along at all.

They all filed into the dining room and filled their plates. Dinner looked delicious and tasted even better. The adults had gathered around the dining table, but the teenagers had drifted out to the terrace. Someone had put on some music and they were eating and dancing, the sound of their voices drifting on the breeze from the open French doors.

Misty finished her dinner and leaned closer to Jared who was talking with Lydia. "I'm going to the restroom. I'll be right back."

"Okay, honey. Are you done with your plate? If not, I won't let them take it."

"I'm done," she assured him. "When I get back, I might get some dessert."

Slipping away from the party, she headed down a hallway that one of the staff had pointed her to instead of going all the way upstairs to her room. She freshened up and then pushed open the door but immediately backed into the bathroom again.

There was a couple kissing in the hallway.

Tom and Taylor.

I did not see that coming.

Tom had to be thirty at least and Taylor had just turned eighteen. Misty also had a strong suspicion that Adam didn't know what his assistant and granddaughter were up to.

They stepped apart and then she heard some whispering, but she couldn't make out what they were saying. She stayed in the bathroom, the door cracked open only slightly until she watched them walk by, disappearing down the hallway. She waited a few moments more to make sure they were really gone and then exited herself, hurrying to get back to the party.

The Reynolds family was certainly interesting, she'd give them that. Did Misty really want to be a part of this clan?

She was beginning to think that answer was a huge no.

When Misty reappeared she had a strange expression, but Jared didn't have a chance to ask her about it because Adam was excitedly telling everyone to gather outside the front door. He had a special birthday surprise for Taylor.

A snazzy sports car. Bright red and gorgeous. The teenagers mobbed the vehicle, oohing and ahhing and pointing out all the cool gadgetry. It could almost drive itself and it parallel parked better than most people.

"Daddy, you're spoiling her," Dahlia protested but not that hard. She was smiling along with everyone else. "The car you gave her for her sixteenth birthday would have been fine for college."

Adam just chuckled and shook his head. "She's worked hard. She deserves it."

David, who hadn't said much in the past few minutes, raised his glass in a sort of salute or toast. "Damn right. Now she's really on the family payroll. As long as she obeys the boss, she can have whatever she wants."

"Go to bed, son. Get some sleep," Adam replied, not even sparing a glance at his son.

Sandra grabbed David by the arm and dragged him inside, her expression thunderous.

"Tom, let's look at those contracts again," Adam said. "I want to settle the language before you go."

"Will do," the other man responded cheerfully, heading back into the house.

"I think I'm going to go upstairs and lie down," Lydia said. "I'm afraid I have a nasty headache. I'll see you all in the morning."

She gave Misty and Jared a friendly smile and also disappeared back into the house. Taylor was now behind the wheel of the car, revving the powerful engine, and Brent was in the passenger seat.

"Taylor, come back inside," Dahlia yelled over the loud motor. "You need to come back inside."

Without even a glance back at her mother, Taylor raced out of the driveway, the red taillights disappearing into the darkness. The other teenagers ran to their own vehicles and quickly followed.

"She never listens," Dahlia said angrily, fumbling in her pocket and pulling out a cell phone. "I'm going to call her and tell her to come back."

"Leave her be, Dee," Adam said. "She shouldn't be answering the phone while she's driving anyway. It's her birthday and she's an adult now."

"She didn't listen to me before."

Dahlia's tone was plaintive, but Adam had already turned back to Misty and Jared. "I need to do a little work but we'll talk more in the morning, right? I'd like to show you both around the grounds. We have horses if you'd like to go for a ride."

They all agreed that sounded like a lovely idea. Misty did want to see more of the area and Jared loved riding.

It appeared that the evening festivities were over, so Misty and Jared went back upstairs to their room. The Reynolds family was…*intense* to say the least and he was relieved for the two of them to be alone again. They could relax and watch some television. He had a feeling that Misty had a great deal to process today, too.

They'd turned down their hallway and were only a few doors from their room when they heard what sounded like the closing of a door and the click of a lock. Jared stopped and looked over his shoulder, but he didn't see anyone.

"Did you hear that?"

"I heard a door. I think."

"I heard it, too." His gaze ran over the hallway. "I thought they said that we were the only ones staying in this part of the house."

She linked her arm with his. "It was probably someone from the staff. I bet it's a lot of work taking care of a place this large."

"That's true. It probably takes a small army to keep this place running."

Back in their own room, they both readied for bed, exhausted after a long day. She'd put on her pajamas and scrubbed her face clean of any cosmetics. She was clicking through the television channels when he exited the en suite bathroom, ready to finally lie down and relax. He found the two phone chargers in his suitcase and went over to the wall socket and plugged them both in, but a light outside and some movement captured his attention. He stepped closer to the window and peered out, surprised at what he was seeing. He blinked a few times to make sure he wasn't mistaken.

Tom. And Dahlia. Embracing in the moonlight. A patio light illuminated the couple. They didn't appear too concerned that they might be seen. Perhaps their relationship wasn't a secret. He and Misty had only met these people today, after all.

But...

"Didn't you say that you saw Tom kissing Taylor earlier?" he asked, turning back to his wife. "Are you sure it was Taylor?"

"I'm positive. They were wearing completely different outfits. Why do you ask?"

"Because I just saw Tom and Dahlia kissing on the back patio. He sure gets around. First the daughter and then the mother. He must be exhausted."

Misty's mouth fell open. "Tom and Dahlia? I guess that's better than Tom and Taylor. Still, it's…weird."

Weird didn't even begin to cover this freak show of a family. That DNA test was probably going to come back negative because his beautiful and loving wife didn't have one thing in common with them. She was like a sheep thrown in with a pack of wolves.

Settling into bed, they watched television for a short while but they were both soon yawning. They'd been up early in the morning for the drive here, so they turned out the lights.

Jared didn't know how long he'd been asleep, but he shot straight up in bed when he heard a bloodcurdling scream from somewhere in the house. It was followed by a second and then a call for help. A woman's voice.

He fumbled with a pair of sweatpants, jerking them on while Misty – who had also heard the screams, pulled on an oversized hoodie over her t-shirt. It easily reached her knees, covering a good portion of her pajama pants. They ran down the stairs toward the woman's voice who was still calling for help. Other doors were flying open and they were joined by Sandra and Dahlia.

"This way," Sandra said, her face pink and her voice breathless. "That's Lydia's voice. It sounds like she's in the library."

She was correct as the door to the library was open and the lights were on. Jared made it to the doorway first and stopped abruptly, his gaze taking in every inch of the scene before him.

Lydia crying loudly, her face buried in her hands.

Adam lying on the floor, a mess of papers around his body and a pool of blood under his head, seeping into the expensive carpet.

Stepping forward, Jared carefully knelt down and pressed his fingers to Adam's neck, trying to find a pulse. He looked up at the three women in the doorway, their expressions of horror almost identical. The news wasn't going to make it any better, but he had to tell them.

"Someone call the police."

It was too late for an ambulance. Adam Reynolds was dead.

CHAPTER NINE

Sheriff Eli Hammond looked like he'd investigated a murder or two in his time. Jared had worked with many small-town cops and it was always obvious when they didn't have a clue how to handle a homicide. For most of them, it was their first and possibly their last as well. A person could read all the police manuals and be at the top of their class, but that didn't mean they'd be a great murder investigator right out of the gate. Some things take practice.

"You seem to be the one in charge here," Sheriff Hammond said to Jared. He'd cordoned off the library with yellow tape and told everyone to stay out as the state forensic team was probably a good two hours away. "How about I ask you a few questions?"

Misty and Jared were sitting with the lawman in the dining room while the others huddled together in the living room. He'd be talking to them eventually as well. Separately. Another sign that Hammond knew what he was doing.

"I am not in charge in any way, shape, or form," Jared replied grimly. "We're simply guests here. We just met Adam Reynolds and his family yesterday. To be honest, I don't know who is in charge."

It certainly wasn't David. No one had found him yet. Lydia, Sandra, and Dahlia were in tears, and Taylor appeared to still be out with her friends. Tom must have gone home at some point.

The sheriff's brow quirked at the response. "Really? You kind of have that air about you. So let's talk anyway. What can you tell me about tonight?"

Jared recounted a brief description of the party, Adam disappearing into the library with Tom for business, and then the screaming hours later.

"It appears that he had a wound on the back of his head and a pool of blood. There was a small gold statue on the ground next to the body. I assume that was the murder weapon. The French doors were open so anyone could have come in or exited. I don't know if there are any security cameras around the house but there's definitely a camera at the gate. Do you have traffic cameras in town? You might want to check those as well."

Oops. Old habits die hard. The sheriff didn't need his help.

"We don't have any traffic cameras," the sheriff said with a small smile. "But I will check the camera at the gate. Anything else?"

Jared shook his head. "Not really. As I said, we don't really know the family well. This was a shock to both of us."

Misty nodded in agreement and Jared tightened his hold around her shoulders. She'd been quiet since realizing Adam Reynolds was dead, and he'd need to talk to her later about how she was feeling. She'd come to this place hoping to find…he didn't really know what she was hoping for, to be honest. She said that she wasn't hoping for a father, but Jared kind of had the feeling that wasn't the case. It wasn't going to happen now, of course.

Sheriff Hammond turned his attention to Misty. "Ma'am, is there anything that you'd like to add? Did you hear anything before the screaming?"

"No," she said softly, leaning closer to Jared. "I was asleep. I think we both were."

"Reynolds said he was going to work in the library with Tom," Jared reiterated. "That's the last time we spoke with him. We went upstairs right after that."

"I'll need to speak with him," Hammond said under his breath. "Also any staff that may have been on duty."

"I'm sure someone can call him for you," Jared replied. "He'll be shocked, of course."

Or not. Tom might have been the last to see Reynolds alive.

"I'm more worried about the press," the sheriff said, snapping the notebook closed. "When they get wind of this, they're going to make my job more difficult. Adam Reynolds was well known in this part of California. He was heavily involved in several charities."

"A rich and successful man probably doesn't have a shortage of people who don't like him," Jared observed, thinking of the research he'd done before they came. Reynolds wasn't well-liked. At all.

"That's very true but luckily for me most of them weren't here last night, although that might change when I get a look at any security footage the estate might have." The sheriff stood so Jared and Misty did as well. It appeared that the interview was over. "Thank you for your time. I'm going to be talking to everyone else as well. I'd ask that you not leave the estate until further notice."

Jared had been expecting the request but that didn't mean that he liked it much. He'd hoped that he and Misty could leave as soon as possible. What they'd come for – getting to know Adam Reynolds – wasn't going to happen now. Plus, Misty was clearly upset about losing her would-be parent. Hanging around wasn't going to help that. He wanted to get her home and in a more comfortable environment so she could begin to deal with all that had happened here this weekend.

But that wasn't going to happen this morning from the looks of things.

"We live in Washington State," Jared stated. "Our young children are staying with friends and we'd like to get back to them as soon as possible."

Polite but firm. That's how he'd said it. Hopefully the local lawman wouldn't take offense.

"I understand, and I hope to get you headed back home as soon as I can. I'm just asking for a little patience. I do appreciate it."

Jared had said almost the exact same words at one point in his career.

They rejoined the group in the living room and Sandra took their place in the dining room with the sheriff.

"What did he ask you?" Dahlia demanded. "What did he want to know?"

Jared shrugged. "He wanted to know about what happened tonight."

"So what did you tell him?"

Misty frowned, her gaze darting between Jared and Dahlia. "The truth, of course. We told him about the dinner party, then that we went to bed and woke up to Lydia screaming."

Upon hearing her name Lydia sobbed again, her face buried in a tissue. She was sitting on the couch, her face tearstained from crying, a highball glass of whiskey at her side.

Dahlia's hand fluttered to her throat, her cheeks pink. "Of course you told him the truth. I just wondered what you said, that's all."

"We couldn't help him much," Jared replied, sinking down

into the couch cushions. He was exhausted and it looked like it was going to be a long day. "We don't know much obviously. Did your father have enemies?"

She nodded vigorously as she sat next to Lydia, patting the crying woman on the shoulder.

"Daddy has made many enemies over the years. There are people that don't wish him well. Do you think he argued with someone? That was blood on the floor, right?"

"It was," Jared confirmed. "It looked like he'd been hit on the back of the head."

Lydia lifted her head, her eyes watery and red. "I think he was hit with the award he won last month. You know, the one the hospital board gave him for donating all that money for a new children's wing. I saw it on the floor next to him."

"Did you hear him talking or arguing with someone?" Dahlia asked Lydia. "Was he meeting with someone tonight?"

"I was in bed. The last person I saw him with was Tom." Lydia groaned and buried her face in the tissue again. "Someone should call Tom. He doesn't know yet."

Dahlia made a face. "My own brother doesn't know yet. He's off getting drunk. Again."

"Has anyone looked for him?" Lydia asked, digging into her robe pocket for a fresh tissue. "We should try and find him. He's going to be so upset."

"When he sobers up," Dahlia said, rolling her eyes. "For all we know, David was the one that Dad argued with."

"Dahlia Elizabeth, you take that back right now."

The voice was from the entrance to the living room. Sandra was already back from talking to the sheriff.

Her daughter, however, didn't seem bothered in the least by her mother's admonishment.

"Don't act so surprised, Mother. You know they hated each

other."

"They didn't hate each other. They simply had very different personalities."

"If you mean that Dad wasn't a drunk loser, then you're right."

The family was starting to turn on each other. This could get ugly fast.

"Why don't I take a look around for David?" Jared offered. "What kind of car does he drive? I can check the garage to see if it's there."

And we can get out of this tension-filled room.

"That's a good idea," Sandra replied, giving Dahlia a reproving look. "He drives a blue BMW sedan. No one else has a car like it."

"We'll go take a look around, then." Jared helped Misty up from the couch. "Is there any place that he usually goes?"

"The local watering hole," Dahlia said, her tone sour. "And when that closes down, he heads out to the barn. Even the horses don't want him there."

"Dahlia," Sandra said in warning. "He's your brother and he has a drinking problem. It's an addiction. He can't control it."

Sighing, Dahlia didn't respond but her expression showed her disgust.

Jared and Misty headed for the front door but there was a deputy stationed there. He held up his hand in a stopping motion when they tried to exit.

"Sorry, folks. I'm not supposed to let anyone out of the house."

The guy, who looked a little rumpled as if someone had woken him up for this murder, was just doing his job. Jared, however, didn't really want to go back into that living room. The Reynolds family had issues. A boatload of them.

"We're actually looking for David Reynolds," Jared said. "No one can find him. I'm sure the sheriff would be interested in his whereabouts, too."

"I am interested in that," Sheriff Hammond said, coming down the staircase. "Why don't we go look for him together? Mike, stay here and make sure no one leaves, okay?"

"Will do, Sheriff."

Hammond held the door open and Jared and Misty followed him out to the front of the house and around to the separate garage on the east side. He stopped at the door, not reaching for the handle.

"Is there anything you want to tell me, Mr. Monroe?"

"I don't think so."

What was this guy going for here? He had a strange look on his face.

"One of my deputies is pretty good with computer stuff. I had him run your name and a whole bunch came up."

Well…shit. He hadn't expected this. But he should have. Hammond wasn't a rookie.

"Yes, I would imagine that would happen."

"My husband doesn't want to talk about Wade Bryson, Sheriff."

His sweet Misty. Always sticking up for him even when she didn't need to. He'd deal with this.

"It's okay, honey." He took a step forward so that he and the sheriff were eye to eye. "If you're looking for a blow-by-blow account then I'm afraid you'll be disappointed. That story is Logan Wright's to tell. I was just helping out a friend. There were a lot of us doing that."

Hammond shook his head. "I don't need to know about Bryson, although I bet it's a hell of a story. No, I'm talking about you. You're a cop. A damn good one if the information my deputy dug out is true. I could use a hand here. We don't get many murders in this little town, and I want to wrap this one up as quickly as possible. I don't want this to get too much press attention, if you know what I mean. I don't need them saying that a podunk sheriff can't find a killer in his own backyard."

That's just what they would say, too. In fact, they'd probably be far more vicious.

"Frankly, I don't need the publicity either, Sheriff."

Hammond smiled and chuckled. "I'd be happy to take all of the credit. And call me Eli, by the way. I think we're going to be good friends."

They might.

"I don't know that I'm looking for any new friends."

"A man can always use friends. Now how about we shake hands and put our heads together on this? You can't tell me that you're not intrigued. That you don't want to investigate this, just a little bit? You can consult. Isn't that what you do?"

Maybe a bit. It was a curious case. It appeared that Adam Reynolds had plenty of enemies right under his own roof.

He glanced down at Misty to see what she thought of all of this, but she was already grinning, barely able to keep her laughter hidden.

"He wants to help, Eli," she said with a smirk. "He just doesn't want to admit it. He loves a mystery and he hates being wrong."

Luckily, I'm not wrong all that often.

"I think it would be good to try and find out who did this," she went on, her expression immediately sobering. "He might be my father, after all. I want him to rest in peace."

Eli's brows shot up. "He might be your father?"

Jared placed his arm around Misty's shoulders, pulling her closer. "It's a possibility and we'd appreciate this not getting in the newspapers."

"Not a problem here. I've kept most of the secrets in this town for more than a decade. My lips are sealed. Now how about we check out the garage for David Reynolds' car?"

"Fine. The sooner we catch the killer, the sooner I can take my wife home."

And get out of this crazy family.

Jared had a bad feeling about all of this. Very, very bad.

CHAPTER TEN

D avid's car was in the garage, but it didn't take long for Jared, Misty, and Eli to find the wayward son. He was passed out on a pool lounger clutching an empty bottle of Captain Morgan to his chest. It was clear that no one had really tried all that hard to find him because it hadn't been difficult. He was less than ten feet from the back patio doors.

Between Jared and Eli they'd been able to wrangle him out of the lounger and into the house, pouring him a cup of coffee and slapping a couple of cold washcloths on the back of his neck to rouse him.

Misty immediately saw scrapes on the man's knuckles. Had he and Adam been in some sort of altercation? They'd been at each other's throats most of the evening.

Tugging at her husband's arm, she pulled him aside. "Did you see...?"

He nodded grimly. "I did. Considering his attitude earlier, I'm not that surprised. Doesn't mean anything, though. He might have punched a raccoon for all we know."

At some point while they'd been looking for David, Taylor had come home and Tom had shown up. The teenager was crying inconsolably while her grandmother Sandra held her. At the moment, Dahlia was regarding her brother with a sour look on her face, ignoring the wails of her daughter.

"You've really done it now, little brother. You killed our father."

David, his head in his hands, shook his head. "I didn't kill anyone. I wouldn't do that."

His tone was plaintive and slightly desperate. He looked up at his mother who had her arm around Taylor. "You believe me, don't you, Mom? I didn't kill Dad."

Eli cleared his throat loudly. "How about I ask the questions? Mr. Reynolds, what do you remember about last evening? When did you last see your father?"

"After dinner. Mom told me to go to bed, but I went outside instead. That's the last time I saw him."

"What happened to your knuckles?" Eli asked, pointing to the scrapes on David's hand. "Looks like you might have got in a fight. Did you and your father argue?"

"No, that didn't happen." David groaned and rubbed at his forehead. He probably had a nasty headache. "I didn't argue with him. I was mad and I punched a wall. That was it."

"What wall?" Jared asked. "Did you leave a mark?"

"Shit, I don't know. I was drunk. I don't even remember exactly where I was. I was outside, that's all I know. I would never hurt my father."

The last was spoken louder, as if saying it at full volume would make everyone believe him.

"But you and your dad had issues?" Eli pressed. "You didn't agree on most subjects."

"I wanted to leave," David sighed, his head hanging again. "I wanted out of this house, but he said he'd cut me off if I left. He wanted to control my life. Hell, he wanted to control everyone's life."

That was motive, albeit not a super strong one. He wasn't alone, though. It didn't say much for Adam, either. He hadn't come off as controlling to her but then she'd only known him a few short hours. Jared's research had painted a far different picture, one that she hadn't liked in the least. She wanted to believe that his terminal illness has changed him but what did she know? Nothing, that's what.

Lydia sniffled into her tissue. "Adam was just a complicated person."

"He was a bastard," Sandra said loudly. "He could be a total jackass and everyone here knows it. I'm honestly surprised it took this long for someone to kill him."

Lydia scowled at Sandra. "Then why are you even here? You divorced him ten years ago."

"I'm here for my children. And I don't have to explain myself to you. For all we know, you killed him yourself. He was getting ready to replace you with a newer model."

"That's not true," Lydia hissed, her cheeks turning bright red. "You don't know anything about me and Adam."

"I know that he had several mistresses when we were married." Sandra shrugged carelessly. "He's never been faithful to anyone. Look at Misty. She's Exhibit A of that. He was cheating on me when I was pregnant with David."

Now it was Misty's turn to be embarrassed. She could feel the heat crawl up her neck as everyone's heads swiveled toward her, waiting for her reply. She really didn't know what to say, though. Sandra wasn't lying. Adam and Annette had been having an affair while he was married. Ugly but true.

"Oh God, leave her alone," Dahlia said in a long-suffering tone. "Poor Misty didn't ask for any of this crap and it's not her fault. She came here because Dad asked her. We all know what he was like. He had faults and some of them made us angry. He had people who hated him. That was no secret. If he cheated on you, Mom, maybe you shouldn't have stayed with him as long as you did. No one forced you not to divorce him. David and I could hear you and Dad arguing all the time. It was a relief when you two separated."

Misty was surprised that it was Dahlia defending her. She'd been under the impression that the other woman wasn't all that fond of her.

"None of this is helpful," Jared cut in, insinuating himself between Misty and the others, his body protecting hers as if he expected them to start throwing things. "Tom, we need to get your statement as well as Taylor's. Everyone else needs to calm down and stop throwing out accusations. That isn't the way to help this investigation."

Taylor finally looked up, her face scrunched up with anger. "Who the fuck are you to tell us to do anything? Go fuck yourself. My grandfather died tonight and you probably killed him."

The teenager had quite the potty mouth but it didn't bother Misty. She'd been known to toss around a few four-letter words when a milder word simply wouldn't do.

Eli held up his hand. "That's enough. Just so you know, Jared is an experienced lawman and I've asked him to help me with this investigation. I'd appreciate your utmost cooperation."

Lifting her chin, Taylor didn't back down. "I meant what I said. There are only two new people here and now my grandfather is dead. I don't think that's a coincidence."

Misty didn't feel the need to defend herself and it wouldn't make any difference anyway. The poor girl was distraught and not thinking clearly. She needed someone to blame, so of course it made sense to pick on any newcomers. They should have expected it.

Sandra pressed a clean tissue into Taylor's hand. "Hush, you're getting all worked up. They didn't kill Adam and you know it."

"They could have," the teenager muttered. "Grandpa's gone."

"Your grandfather made a lot of enemies," David said. "Everyone but you and Lydia hated him."

"That's not true," Taylor shot back. "Lots of people loved him."

"Name five," David laughed. "I could name more than a couple dozen who thought he was a son of a bitch. I could name at least ten people whose lives he ruined. Face it, Adam Reynolds only loved himself. The minute you stepped out of line he would have come down on you. It was only a matter of time."

Taylor looked up at her mother. "Mom, make him take it back. It's not true."

To her credit Dahlia appeared conflicted, not quite ready to jump to her father's defense but not ready to condemn him, either. "Your grandfather was a complicated man."

That wasn't the answer that Taylor was looking for. She burst into tears again, cuddling closer to her grandmother.

"I think my daughter makes a good point, though," Dahlia went on. "How do you know for sure that Jared didn't do this? He could be helping you frame an innocent person."

"My husband didn't do this," Misty protested, finally finding her voice. "And neither did I. I came here to get to know Adam. I wouldn't kill him. That doesn't make any sense."

"That's enough," Eli said firmly. "I'd like to speak with Tom in the dining room, please. Taylor, then I'll speak with you."

Tom, who had been quiet this entire time stood up quickly,

only glancing at Dahlia briefly. Anyone else wouldn't have noticed it but Misty did, especially after Jared had seen them kissing just hours before.

"I'm happy to help in any way I can, Sheriff."

"Then follow me." Eli paused for a moment. "I just want to address your question, Dahlia, as to why I don't think Jared and Misty killed your father. It's because Jared Monroe is considered one of the best lawmen in this country. If he was planning to kill your father, he wouldn't have done it so sloppily. He would have done it in a way that no one would ever have known, and he would have made it look like an accident. That's how I know. The person that did this was an amateur."

With that, Eli strode into the dining room, Tom trying to keep up. That left Misty and Jared with a roomful of people that may or may not be inclined to like them all that much. It was an uncomfortable feeling and it reminded her of growing up in Fielding. The town residents hadn't been all that supportive of Misty since she was the daughter of the town tramp. She'd been teased, bullied, and ostracized through most of her formative years. It was only after marrying Jared that she'd been able to deal with her tormenters. He'd given her the self-confidence to thumb her nose at the busybodies in a small town.

But this was no small town, and these weren't the pious and gossipy members of the Ladies Auxiliary. These people might be family.

And that was a mighty depressing thought indeed.

CHAPTER ELEVEN

Jared was drinking a hot cup of coffee on the back patio when Eli came out to join him. He sat at the table, a bottle of water in his hand.

"I've known these people for almost a decade, and I can say without a doubt that any one of them is capable of this under the right conditions," Eli said, settling back into the chair. "Adam was not a well-liked man."

"We've been here less than twenty-four hours, but we've already seen quite a bit of animosity between them, although I have to say that Adam Reynolds has been nothing but nice to Misty and I. But then we only knew him for a few hours."

"Where is your wife? Is she okay? I would imagine she's taking this hard."

"She went upstairs to lie down and get some rest. I do think she's upset but she tends to keep things to herself because she doesn't want to bother anyone," Jared sighed. "I also think she's confused about the whole situation. Frankly, I would be too."

"My late wife was the same. Didn't want to be a bother. Even when she was sick, she'd just say that she was fine. Never wanted to complain."

Eli wasn't all that old. Maybe in his forties?

"I'm sorry for your loss."

"Cancer three years ago," the sheriff replied with a grimace. "She fought long and hard but eventually… Anyway, she was a wonderful wife and I was lucky to have her for as long as I did."

"I feel the same way about Misty."

"She seems like a fine woman. Not sure how she'd fit in with this group. They're all a little bloodthirsty but it's really not their fault. Adam brought them up that way. Wanted them to compete with one another."

That was something Jared knew a great deal about. He'd been brought up the same way but luckily it hadn't been quite as intense. He'd never murdered a sibling over it.

"Sounds like you know them well."

Chuckling, Eli nodded his head. "Adam Reynolds was the type that thought that the local police worked for him and him alone. I told him once that I worked for the taxpayers of this town and he told me that he paid the most taxes by far so that meant that he was my boss. He told me that the mayor, my real boss, would agree with him."

Small towns and politics. Never a dull moment. Jared didn't miss it in the least.

"Did you ever ask the mayor about it?"

"I did. He told me to keep Adam Reynolds happy and that no one else really mattered. He also said that if I told anyone that he'd said that, he'd deny it."

"Is he still the mayor?"

"He is. He runs unopposed every two years."

"You know, a friend of mine had an issue like that. His wife convinced him to run for mayor and he won. First thing he did was run the old crooked mayor out of town. Turns out the townsfolk were just as tired of all the bullshit as he was."

Tanner was making several changes in Springwood and the town had never been more prosperous. He was a shoo-in to be reelected.

"That might be something I could do," Eli conceded. "Especially now that Adam has passed on. None of his children want to stay in the area. I suspect they'll sell the house and land."

"Probably to some developer who will divide it up and build condos."

"They call it progress." There was a small pause before Eli continued. "Adam was sick. I don't know if he told you."

"I knew. That's why he reached out to Misty. To make amends. He said he wanted to fix some of the bad things he'd done in his life."

"Now that would be quite a task."

"That's pretty much what he said. He told us that he'd done some awful things in his life."

"Possibly illegal as well."

Jared rubbed at his chin, stubbled since he hadn't shaved today. He needed to get upstairs and clean up, but he didn't want to miss the forensic team when they arrived. "Is that where you're leaning? You think this might be a business deal gone bad?"

"I don't know. It's a possibility. Lord knows his own family had plenty of motive. What do you think? Any observations?"

"I have more questions than answers," Jared replied. "For example, last night Sandra and Lydia seemed very friendly to one another. Like friends. Today they're blaming each other for murder. What's up with that? And also, David apparently has a drinking problem and hated his father. What's the history there? As for Dahlia, I'm not sure. She seems fine, as does Taylor. Hell, she's just a kid. Tom is a possibility since I doubt working for Reynolds was any sort of treat. It was probably hell. He was also the last to see the deceased as far as I know."

Eli leaned forward, his elbows propped on the table. "Sandra and Lydia usually do get along just fine. They're not friends, though. Those two are far too competitive for that. I sure as hell don't think Sandra ever wanted Adam back so she was no threat to Lydia. Lydia, on the other hand, was pressing Adam for a wedding ring which he was absolutely not going to give her. He'd told her and anyone who would listen as much."

That wasn't the greatest motive for murder, though. If Lydia killed Adam then she'd never get to marry him. If he'd been cheating that was a whole other kettle of fish. He'd seen people shot for just looking at the opposite sex. Jealousy could get ugly.

"I know he wasn't exactly the faithful type in his youth. Did he get any better there in these last years?"

"There have always been rumors. I will say that Adam never flaunted his relationships."

"So he was only half an asshole?"

Eli laughed. "No, he was a total asshole, but his womanizing isn't what put him over the top."

"How did he feel about his ex-wife?"

"That relationship was far more complicated. It cost him big bucks when they divorced. They didn't have a prenup and Adam was pissed as hell that he basically had to give her half. She did convince him that staying close for the kids' sake was important."

"How close?" Jared asked. "She spent the night here. Is that normal?"

Eli shook his head. "She has her own house on the estate, but she spends most of her time in San Francisco. She told me she only spent the night because it was late and she didn't want to drive back to her place. She says she does that from time to time."

"Sounds like they didn't hate each other then."

"I think he mostly tolerated her because she was active in several philanthropic endeavors. He wanted people to think he was just as involved but basically he only signed the checks. Day to day involvement wasn't of interest to him. He and Sandra didn't spend much time together or anything even before the divorce from what I heard, but that was before my time. The only person he openly adored was Taylor, and she loved her grandmother so he wasn't about to push Sandra out."

"His granddaughter seemed genuinely heartbroken about Adam."

"They were close. He was so damn proud of her. He told me that once she finished college, he was going to start turning over the business to her a little at a time. Of course, that was years away. She just graduated high school. She's a smart one, though. Her boyfriend Brent is supposed to be some sort of genius as well. I think his father is some sort of pharmaceutical researcher. Any other observations?"

Jared drained his coffee cup. "Sandra was dressed for bed. She was wearing a robe and slippers. Dahlia, on the other hand, was still in her clothes and had her makeup on. It was hard to tell with Lydia. She'd changed from dinner, but she wasn't necessarily dressed for bed."

She'd been wearing a light blue sweatsuit, but like Jared, she might have pulled it on to go check on Adam.

"That goes along with Sandra's story that she was upstairs asleep from ten o'clock on. Dahlia said she was also asleep, though."

"In her clothes? Interesting. What did Lydia say?"

"She said that she was upstairs asleep and at one point she woke up and realized that Adam hadn't come to bed yet, so she went looking for him. In his office, of course. That's when she found him on the floor and screamed for help."

"Sounds plausible," Jared remarked. "I don't sleep well without Misty so I can see her being restless. It's Dahlia's story that I'm questioning, although I suppose she could have been watching television and fallen asleep in a chair or something. She might not have had a chance to change or take off her makeup."

"First thing my Debra did when she got home was take off her bra and makeup. But maybe she was unique."

"Actually, that's what Misty does too," Jared replied. "But like you, I don't know if they're alone in that. Let's just say that I think Dahlia needs to be looked at. Along with David. His alibi sucks. Do you know why he hated his old man so much?"

"Once again this was all before my time, but the rumor is that David wanted to be an artist or something like that. Adam wanted him to go into the family business. Apparently, it all blew up when David graduated and ran away with some girl and got married in Las Vegas. Adam made him annul the marriage and dump the girl. David never forgave him. He has a job with the family business but supposedly hasn't shown up for work in years. Stays here and lives off daddy's money and gets drunk every day."

"Hell of a way to live your life. Did it occur to him to just leave?"

"I'm sure that it did but then he'd have to give up the money. Dahlia, on the other hand, did exactly what Adam wanted her to. Got her business degree, married the guy that was picked out for her, had an heir, and didn't complain. The only deviation from the plan was when she got divorced, but by then Adam had Taylor so he didn't care."

Jared had done a great deal of research into Adam Reynolds, but this was stuff that wasn't in databases. He knew bank accounts and investments holdings. He knew that Adam liked to eat at expensive restaurants and wear bespoke suits – the credit cards told him that – but this was information that only an insider would know.

It also made him hopeful that Misty wasn't related to Reynolds in any way. The family was a shitshow and the farther away they were the better.

"The more I learn about Adam Reynolds the less I like him. But here's the thing…he was a dying man. Why on earth would anyone go to the trouble of killing him if he was going to die shortly anyway? It doesn't make a damn bit of sense to me."

"To me either," Eli agreed. "Which makes me think this crime wasn't thought through."

"Spur of the moment decision? An argument?"

"Possibly. David's knuckles were grazed. Once the forensic team and the coroner get here, we'll know more. I'm not allowed to touch the body until they're done, and I know you're too well-trained to mess with a body or a crime scene."

"Then let's hope they get here soon. In the meantime, how about we check the security camera at the gate?"

"Good idea."

Jared jerked his head toward the house. "What about all of them? Are we just going to leave them here?"

"They'll be fine. Mike will make sure no one leaves. Besides, I think letting them stew a little bit won't hurt. They'll be thinking about the questions that they've already answered and the ones I might ask later."

That was the problem. Too many questions and very little answers.

Who would kill a dying man?

Chapter Twelve

Misty's eyes were gritty when she woke up, disoriented for a moment as to where she was. It took her a few seconds to remember that she was at Adam Reynolds' home, in a guest room, and that he'd been murdered at some point last night.

It hadn't been a nightmare, although she'd hope that it was. The high hopes she'd had when she'd come here yesterday had crashed hard.

"Hey, babe. Are you awake now?"

How long had Jared been standing in the middle of their room watching her stare blankly at the windows? She'd been so out of it she hadn't even seen him.

Rubbing her eyes, she groaned and stretched. "Not completely, if I'm being perfectly honest. How long did I sleep? What year is it?"

"You slept hard," Jared replied with a gentle smile. "You've been out about two hours. I didn't want to wake you. Obviously, you needed the sleep."

"What about you? You don't need the sleep?"

"I'm used to being sleep deprived, remember? Are you hungry? The cook put out some food. I can go and fill you a plate."

The thought of food made her stomach twist. Not in a good way.

"I think I'll pass. Food doesn't sound appetizing to me right now."

Jared came to sit on the edge of the bed, his hand reaching out to smooth some of the hair back out of her eyes. It probably looked like a rat's nest, but he was too polite to say anything.

"Do you want to talk about it?"

"Not really. Adam is gone and I'm never going to get a chance to get to know him. I had so many questions for him about my mother. He told me that we'd talk about all of that today, but of course, that's not going to happen now. This whole trip...it feels like it's been a waste."

"You did get to meet him."

She pulled her knees to her chest and wrapped her arms around them. "It's almost worse in a way. Before he contacted me I was doing fine and living my life. Then everything got turned upside down and I thought... Damn, I don't know what I thought, to be honest."

"You thought you were going to have a father. I think that's a pretty normal hope, honey."

Had she thought that? Perhaps, but not really. It hadn't been about that. She'd known in her heart that it was far too late. Then what had she hoped for?

"I don't think that I wanted him as a father. I think I wanted...answers."

Jared's fingers stroked her cheek softly, his fingers rough and soothing at the same time.

"I'm not sure that Adam had those. We don't even really know if he was telling the truth."

"And we'll never know now."

"No, we won't, but thinking that you would have managed

to get answers from him would be quite optimistic. He wasn't a good person. He's lied and cheated and just generally been a horrible person. He wasn't anyone that you could count on."

"I know that he wasn't a good man, but in the few hours that I had with him, he was nice to me."

Chuckling, Jared leaned down and brushed his lips over hers, sending tingles straight to her toes. She marveled that after all of these years he could still so easily get her attention.

"You set the bar pretty damn low for him. All he had to do was not be a jackass for three hours. I would imagine anyone could do that. Although judging by the family down-stairs…maybe not."

Giggling, she snuggled closer to her husband. "They are kind of a handful, aren't they? I doubt we'll ever see them again after we leave here. I don't think they're people that I care to spend much more time with."

"Hallelujah, I was afraid you were going to tell me that you wanted to have a relationship with them. Honey, the sooner we leave here the better."

She settled against his larger frame, her head pillowed on his chest so she could drink in his strength. "I think I'm going to have to agree with you. Did you and Eli make any progress?"

"Yes and no. The forensic team finally made it and they're downstairs now with the coroner. Eli and I compared notes and so far, there are a shit ton of suspects just in this house. Add in the open French doors and it's anyone's guess who did this."

"Did you see the gate footage yet?"

"Eli is getting it now. If you want, you can come downstairs and watch it with us. He's set up a sort of command center for this in the butler's pantry."

Misty quickly freshened up and then she and Jared made their way downstairs. Not surprisingly, the group in the living room had dispersed with Dahlia, Sandra, Taylor, Brent, and Tom eating in the dining room. There was no sign of Lydia or David. Misty assumed the latter was sleeping off his hangover.

It was interesting to see Tom, Taylor, and Dahlia all in the same room together. It didn't appear that Taylor knew about Tom and Dahlia, nor did Brent know about Taylor and Tom.

They found Eli in the butler's pantry, a laptop on the small table in front of him. He waved them in and then asked them to shut the door.

"I think it's probably best if those out there don't know that we're looking at this footage until after I know what we're dealing with."

"Did you find any more security cameras?" Jared asked.

"No, Adam was vehemently anti-technology. He always said that living way out here was security enough, but strangely when he traveled he always had a huge bodyguard with him. His logic didn't make much sense."

"None of this makes any sense," Misty remarked. "Adam was ill. He would have died within six months. They didn't need to kill him."

"Unless they wanted him dead now and not later," Eli replied, cueing up the video. "I think we need to look into his business dealings. Was he planning on making any big changes? Perhaps someone didn't want him to do that."

"I'll get working on that," Jared said. "You're right, we need to know what Adam was doing in the weeks leading to his death."

"I've cued up the video to begin at dinner time."

As with most security footage, it was rather boring and not the best quality. Misty watched as Brent, Taylor, and her friends drove into the estate, then later Tom arrived. There was a long portion where nothing happened and then Taylor and her friends drove out again. This time she was driving her new car and her friends trailed behind her, including Brent, in their own vehicles. A while later Tom drove out as well and then the last of the household staff. Then there was nothing until the police arrived.

"I don't think that helps much," Misty said with a sigh. "It doesn't show anything that we didn't already know."

"It confirms their stories," Eli replied. "That's important."

"And there is no back way into the estate?" Jared queried. "No way they could have circumvented the cameras?"

"There's no back gate as such," Eli explained. "But if they're willing to climb and get dirty they certainly could have gotten in. Adam had a fence around most of the estate and the property backs up into a mountain. It's not impenetrable."

"Where does that leave us?" Misty asked.

"We start with the most obvious suspects. His family. They were all already here. No one had to climb a fence or a mountain to get to him. Those open French doors could have been a ruse by the killer to throw us off and make us look at other people." Eli shifted in his chair. "I know you probably don't want to hear this, but has it occurred to you that Adam was killed this weekend specifically because you were here? Two outsiders visiting. You're the perfect people to blame this on."

"It had occurred to me," Jared said grimly. "And it wouldn't surprise me. I wouldn't trust this family as far as I could throw them."

This seemed so...farfetched. Could it be true?

Misty rubbed at a throbbing temple. She needed some ibuprofen and some caffeine. She also wouldn't mind going back in time about twenty-four hours. "You think that the killer is trying to frame us for Adam's murder?"

"We'll see. Forensics should be finishing up soon. Maybe

we'll get some answers."

Answers would be good. So far, they had too many questions and too many suspects.

Who killed Adam and why?

Misty had a feeling it wasn't as straightforward as they'd hoped.

While they waited for forensics to report to Eli, Jared went out by the pool for a little privacy so he could call his partners, Logan Wright and Jason Anderson. He'd briefly sent a text regarding what had happened, and they'd asked him to call with more information when he had a chance.

"I'm calling but I'm not sure that I have any information yet. We're waiting on the coroner and the forensics team," he reported to Jason. Logan was out working another case and would be briefed later. "It's a head scratcher but it really shouldn't be. Honestly, this should be an easy case."

"I'm listening," Jason replied. "I know the basics. Your possible father-in-law was murdered last night. Do you know how he died yet?"

"Not officially, but from what I could see it was blunt force trauma to the back of the head."

They reviewed a few other key points in the case before Jason got down to the crux of the matter.

"You think it's mighty strange that a dying man was killed."

"He probably would have passed on within six months if what he said about his cancer was true. I think Eli has a good theory. There's a reason that Adam Reynolds had to die now and not later."

"Could be business. Could be personal. Did any of the family say he was talking about changing his will? That might spur them into action."

"No one has said anything and believe me when I say that if he was talking about that they would. They don't bother to hide their animosity to one another."

"I'll take your word for it. I'll start digging into Reynolds' businesses. See if he's pissed anyone off lately."

"Good luck. From my research he regularly made enemies and didn't give a shit about it."

"Sounds like a real charmer. How's Misty holding up? She has to be devastated, going up there to meet her father and then him being murdered."

"She's hanging in there. She's upset, of course, but she's a strong woman. Eli did mention also that the reason Adam was killed this weekend was so that Misty and I could be framed for the murder."

"I could see that, but it sounds like it isn't working. Call or text me when you have more from forensics. What they find might close the case easily."

"You're such a damn optimist."

"That's me. A born optimist. Listen, be careful. There's a good chance that a killer is running around that house. You don't want to get their attention."

"It might be too late."

Jared spoke with Jason for a few minutes and then ended the call. He began to slip his phone into his pocket but then paused, remembering how heartbroken Misty had looked this morning. She needed her family more than ever right now. He punched in his brother Ty's contact and waited for him to pick up.

"Hey, aren't you supposed to be on vacation for a few days? Not that I'm not glad to hear from you."

Leave it to Ty to not even say hello, just launching into the conversation. Jared was close to both of his brothers, but he'd always felt a special connection to Ty. Sadly, he and his sister Becky didn't get along so well. She was nasty to Misty and for Jared that was a hard boundary. Until she could act civilly, she wasn't welcome in their lives.

"We are on vacation but let's just say that it hasn't exactly worked out the way we wanted it to."

"What happened? Are you stranded somewhere? Do I need to call out a posse?"

Jared quickly filled in his brother on what had happened, omitting the part about the possibility of being framed for murder.

"Shit, poor Misty," Ty said when he heard the story. "To think she almost had found her father and then had him yanked away so soon. That sucks."

"That's why I'm calling you. You and Misty are the closest in the family and I was wondering if you might give her a call. I'm here for her but I want to remind her that she does have a family that loves her. This has all been so hard on her."

"Absolutely, I'll call her," Ty promised. "We adore her and I'll make sure she knows that. But I'm not so sure that it's going to do the trick, bro. Kyle and I can't make up for not having a parent, as much as we'd like to. You know that as well as I do."

At those words from his brother, Jared felt himself shutting down. He simply didn't want to deal with it. He'd first lost his mother several years ago before meeting Misty, and then his father less than a year ago. The wound was too fresh. He'd decided not to think about it and so far, it had worked.

"Thanks for talking to Misty." Jared ignored the elephant in the phone call. "I think it will really make her feel better."

He and Ty ended their call and Jared tucked the phone away in his pocket. His father Gerald Monroe was a big believer in sucking it up, staying quiet, and not making a messy display of emotions. If it was good enough for his dad, it was good enough for him. He was fine; it was Misty that needed the support. He had everything under control. Including himself.

✧ ✧ ✧ ✧

Eli caught Jared a few minutes later on the way upstairs. "I talked to the coroner and the head forensics guy. None of this is official, of course, but the coroner said that it does appear that Adam Reynolds died from blunt force trauma. Since Adam had a great deal of notoriety, he's going to run every test known to man to make sure we cover every single detail, though. He's going to do the autopsy first thing in the morning. Being rich and murdered puts you straight to the head of the line, apparently."

Those were the kind of perks Jared could do without.

"What about forensics? Did they find anything?"

"They pulled some fingerprints off of the statue and around the office, and one particularly promising palm print on the inside glass of the French doors. They also found a button on the floor, a small round white one like off a shirt, but they don't know if it was there before the murder. It could have been. According to Lydia, people are in and out of Adam's office quite a bit, including the staff."

"About the staff, are we overlooking any of them? Should we be looking in that direction?"

"I did talk to them but they had all left for the evening. They don't live on the property."

"So we maybe have prints and a button."

A button probably wasn't going to help much but fingerprints could definitely solve a case.

"We'll hear about the prints tomorrow as well. Until then, I've told the family not to leave town."

The way Eli was looking at Jared…

"And that goes for us too, I suppose? I just want to get Misty out of here. This place isn't good for her."

Or me.

"I'm just asking you to stick around another day or two. You weren't planning on leaving until Monday anyway, right?"

That was true, but…

"We'd planned to have some fun looking around the area."

"Then do that. I'm not asking you to be stuck here in the house."

Would Misty even be in the mood to do anything enjoyable? On the other hand, a simple drive or walk might be just the thing. Get her out of the house and breathe in some fresh air.

Away from the Reynolds family.

"I might try and take her for a walk. We need to get out of this house. I'm going stir crazy here."

With that idea in his head Jared sought out Misty, finding her reading a book in their room.

"Let's get out of here for a little while. Go for a walk. We both need a little space from all of this bullshit."

For a moment, he thought she might argue with him but then she tossed her book aside and gave him the first real smile he'd seen all day.

"Take me away."

CHAPTER THIRTEEN

Misty hadn't realized just how tense she was until they were out of that house. She was an introvert by nature and being around that many people was exhausting. Add in their generally unhappy demeanors and it drained the life out of her.

The sun was shining, however, and the weather mild. She was holding Jared's hand as they walked around the grounds, the house a speck in the distance. The fresh air was working wonders for her own mood, and she could tell that her husband was feeling it too. He looked more content than he had since they'd arrived.

"This walk was just what I needed," she said, giving his hand a squeeze.

"Me too. It's like that house has a gray cloud over the top of it."

"To be fair, a person did just die."

"They were like that before," Jared scoffed. "Especially David. It was clear he hates that house and his dad."

Misty hated to think that any of Adam's own family killed him. She desperately wanted it to be someone who had snuck into the house and wasn't related to him in any way.

"Lydia seemed pretty happy last night. So did Sandra. And Taylor, of course."

Jared's lips quirked up into a smile. "It was her birthday and she got a car. That would have made me happy at eighteen."

"What did you get at eighteen?"

"A job," Jared chuckled. "I spent the summer delivering groceries around Fielding, in addition to working on the ranch, so I'd have pocket money at college in the fall. Dad didn't let any of us lounge around over the summer. Not even Becky."

It was only a flicker. A sadness that flitted across Jared's features but was gone as quickly as it had come. Most people wouldn't even have caught it, but Misty had been studying her husband's face for years now. Even if she wasn't his wife, as an artist should would have found his square jaw and bluer than blue eyes fascinating. But as his spouse, she'd found that she had to pay close attention. He was a master at pushing down his emotions, pretending that they weren't even there. That was his father's doing. Gerald Monroe hadn't been much for messy displays of any emotion, even the happy ones. He'd been all about control and that's what he'd taught his sons.

Jared had certainly internalized that lesson even if he verbalized that he didn't agree with it. He never told Nate that boys don't cry. He never tried to coach either of their children to *suck it up and don't let it show*. He completely agreed that his father's parenting philosophy might have a few flaws.

But...

He wasn't always successful in overcoming almost forty years of Monroe-family programming. Today was one of those moments.

"You're thinking about Gerald."

She didn't phrase it as a question because she didn't want to give Jared the chance to deny it.

"Not really. Just thinking about my childhood for a short moment. I can do that without thinking about Dad."

Misty couldn't imagine how he could do that. It was taking compartmentalization a bit too far.

The fact was…since Gerald's death her husband had been acting like this. He'd allowed himself to grieve until the funeral was over and then he'd acted like he was over it. That he'd mourned and had moved on. He'd even said, "Life has to go on, honey. That's what Dad would have wanted."

Knowing Gerald Monroe, Misty couldn't argue that but what he wasn't seeing is that he was using a bunch of unhealthy coping mechanisms to deal with all of this. Basically, denial. He was acting as if losing his father wasn't a big deal anymore.

"I would imagine that you do think about him sometimes. I think about my mom and she's been gone even longer."

Misty's relationship with her mother had been complicated to say the least, but she never shied away from thoughts about her parent. Good, bad, and in between. They were her life and pretending anything different wasn't being genuine. The strange thing was Jared was one of the most honest people she'd ever met in her life.

To other people.

To himself? Not so much.

"Sometimes."

She tugged at his hand, pausing on the small path they were following so he too had to stop.

"You don't have to not talk about your father just because I lost mine last night."

He was shaking his head before she even finished the sentence. "That's not it at all. I just don't find it helpful to talk about the past all that much. That's it."

"Okay, I was just chatting about it. It's not a big deal."

"I didn't say it was a big deal."

He sounded defensive which was the last thing she wanted him to feel. He'd been happy thirty seconds ago and she wanted to get back to that state. This wasn't the time or place to try and get him to open up about his feelings. Jared Monroe wouldn't do that until he was damn good and ready to. So she changed the subject.

"I talked to Reed and Kaylee and the kids while you were downstairs. They're going to have a movie night and eat pizza and popcorn."

"I doubt they miss us at all," Jared laughed. "Soon they're going to start suggesting weekend getaways for us just so they can hang out with Reed and Kaylee. Hell, I think the dog even likes Kaylee more than me."

"She does give them cheese," Misty reminded him. "But our pets love their daddy no matter what."

Jared nodded toward a shady spot under some trees. "How about there? It looks plenty quiet and secluded."

It did and she easily agreed, helping him spread out the blanket. They both sat down and Misty opened up the small basket, taking out the bread, cheese, wine, and fruit. For the first time today she was hungry. It was amazing what fresh air and good company could do. She and Jared didn't get much alone time in their hectic lives, so she wanted to enjoy every moment of this.

He poured the chilled wine into paper cups. "How about we make a toast?"

She accepted her glass and raised it. "I think that's a great idea. What should we toast to?"

"To us? To five minutes to ourselves? To happiness?"

She'd drink to all of that. "To us, five minutes, and happiness. Do you think we could get a little more than five minutes though?"

"We might even get fifteen if we're lucky."

The wine was cold and fruity on her tongue and she savored the flavor. Jared popped a grape into his mouth while she tore off a piece of bread from the baguette. They ate in silence for a few minutes until most of the food was gone.

"I can't believe I ate all of that," she marveled. "I wasn't even hungry."

There wasn't much left but an apple and a few grapes. Every bit of the bread and cheese was gone along with half a bottle of wine. Misty's tummy was full and she was more content than she'd been in a long time. Since that letter had arrived, her world had been turned upside down.

"You needed to eat," Jared replied gently. "Starving yourself won't change the situation."

No, it wouldn't. But sometimes it was hard to be practical and level-headed.

"The fresh air was just what I needed. I didn't realize how stuffy and oppressive the house was."

"Amen to that. I'm glad you feel better."

Yawning widely, Misty sank back on the blanket, letting her eyelids flutter closed. She was so tired. She might be able to sleep for days. Jared situated himself next to her so her head could pillow on his shoulder. Before long she'd fallen asleep, lulled by the steady rise and fall of her husband's chest.

The sun was still high in the sky when she awoke sometime later to Jared's fingers tickling her ribcage under her cotton t-shirt. He was stroking the sensitive skin softly, making her giggle even though she was still half-asleep.

"What are you doing, handsome?"

"I'm not doing anything. It's you that was doing something."

"I was just lying here sleeping."

"Exactly. You know how I get when we cuddle."

She certainly did. Jared might not be a talker, but he was happy to let his body handle all of his communication. He loved to snuggle and nine times out of ten it led to more.

Shifting on the blanket, she could feel his erection pressing against her hip. "Are you serious? You want to have sex out here?"

"Since when do you not like having sex outdoors? That's our thing."

He had a point. Since the beginning of their relationship, they'd taken "it" outdoors as often as possible but only at the family cabin on their remote property. Then she could be sure no one was going to be taking a stroll and discovering them...naked.

"Anyone could walk by."

Looking up, he frowned and shook his head. "We're far from the house and the path. No one is going to see us. And even if they did, they'd just be jealous as hell."

"This is how you sweet talk me into public fornication?" Misty laughed. "Try another tactic."

"Okay, how about this?"

That devil of a man rolled over so he was hovering above her, his all too skilled lips blazing a path from right below her ear down to that spot on the back of her neck that made her a quivering mass of jelly.

Did I mention that my eyes roll back in my head too?

He nibbled at her collarbone, his mouth pushing aside the neckline of her shirt and exposing a shoulder. Of their own volition her hands dug into his muscular shoulders as pleasure ricocheted around her body like a pinball machine. A heat began to build in her belly, the warmth spreading all the way to her curled toes.

Sliding down her body, his big hands tugged her t-shirt over her body, and she lifted up to help him remove it as well as her blue jeans. She wanted them out of the way; the temperature outside had risen in the last few minutes, turning a mild California day into a tropical day at the beach. Her panties followed quickly, adding to the pile of clothes next to them.

Her own hands glided under his t-shirt to the warm, smooth skin underneath. Her fingers traced his ribs and then over his impossibly flat abdomen to come to rest at his button fly. She traced the outline of his cock, dragging a groan from his lips as he reached down and unfastened his jeans.

"Easy honey, we'll get there."

But they weren't getting there fast enough. Her husband was taking his sweet time, pressing open-mouthed kissed to her stomach, moving lower inch by inch and driving her slowly out of her mind.

The world spun on its axis when his mouth found her swollen button and he pressed two fingers inside of her. They slid in easily as she was primed and ready, but as usual Jared Monroe had to be in charge. Her nails dug onto his biceps, urging him to hurry. She needed him now. A coil of arousal had formed in her belly and was tightening painfully with every swipe and swirl of his genius tongue.

"Jared," she said sucking in a breath, her lids too heavy to hold open. "Now…"

"Not yet. You first."

"Bossy."

"Can't disagree. Now come for me, sweetheart."

His thumb flicked back and forth insistently over her clit and a shiver ran down her spine. A sigh escaped her lips as the pressure built upon itself exponentially until the dam finally broke. Hot lava ran through her veins and her body bowed off of the blanket, but his gentle hands held her safely as she allowed the rivers of pleasure to flood her senses.

He moved up her body, pressing her thighs farther apart and positioning himself exactly where she wanted him. With one thrust he was deep inside and for a moment her breath caught at the beauty of being this close to her husband. So amazingly good, and it just kept getting better.

Jared had barely allowed her to come down from her climax before he was sending her higher once again, their bodies moving in a primal rhythm that they'd perfected long ago. She knew this man so well. What he'd do if she touched him just there…or there. How he'd react or groan or moan if her lips brushed the cords of his neck or nibbled at the damp flesh of his shoulder. He loved it when she dug her nails into his bare back and wrapped her legs around his waist. He adored it when she whispered his name in his ear along with any dirty suggestions she might come up with along the way.

To others it might have felt old hat but to her it felt safe, familiar, and exciting. She could be herself and not have to worry about anything but the magic that they made together.

Her second orgasm was no less intense than the first, throwing her into a star-spangled universe that spun and tilted around her. Jared followed her over the cliff, her name on his lips as he thrust inside of her one last time and stayed there, his body tense and straining before collapsing on top of her. They giggled, cuddling together, her head on his chest and her body curved into his. She could hear his heartbeat under her ear, strong and steady.

Like Jared himself.

Eventually, the air cooled and they quickly dressed, packing up their belongings and heading back to the house. Misty's steps slowed the closer they came to the imposing edifice. She had to admit that she wasn't all that thrilled about going back. She wanted Jared and Eli to find the person that murdered Adam, but it wasn't easy living among the suspects.

Even if every single one of them was innocent, they were still difficult people to be around. She'd love to sleep in her own bed tonight, knowing that her children were tucked in just down the hall. She missed the sound of their voices and their warm hugs and kisses before bedtime.

As they approached the back patio, they could hear raised voices and see Dahlia, Taylor, Sandra, and Eli standing next to the pool. Dahlia's arms were gesturing wildly and Taylor was crying.

"Does it make me a bad person if I tell you that I kind of want to turn around and go back to where we came from?" Misty asked with a sigh. She wasn't used to this much drama. "I'm a horrible person. Just awful."

"You're not a horrible person. Why don't you slip upstairs and I'll help Eli with whatever this is. You don't have to deal with it."

That sounded like heaven but she couldn't let Jared do this on his own.

"Nope, I'm the reason we're here this weekend. I'm not abandoning ship."

The voices were louder as they grew closer. Dahlia's face was red and so was Sandra's. Taylor was sobbing, her face swollen from the tears.

"I've got two men checking out that area," Eli said, his voice loud but calm. "I always have a man watching the gate. If anyone is on the estate, they'll find them."

Shaking her head, Dahlia dashed at a few tears that were rolling down her own cheeks.

"Like you've found the person that killed my father? He ended up dead, Sheriff. My daughter and myself could have been killed today. Do you understand that?"

"I understand perfectly well and I'm doing all I can."

Eli turned to Jared, an expression of relief on his face. "There you are. We were worried about both of you."

"I told you that we were going for a walk and a picnic."

"A picnic?" Sandra repeated, her voice shrill. "You were on a picnic while my daughter and granddaughter were almost killed. We thought that perhaps you were both dead as well."

Jared held up his hands in a stop motion. "Can we stop a second here and rewind? I think we've missed a significant portion of this conversation. This is the first we've heard that anyone had an attempt on their life."

Eli nodded in agreement. "You're right. You have missed the beginning. Apparently, Dahlia and Taylor were horseback riding back on the trails and they heard three shots being fired. Dahlia's horse is a little jumpy and he took off, so Taylor went off after her mother to try and catch them, slow them down. She did eventually and now my guys are combing the trails looking for whomever might have shot at them."

Another murder attempt? Holy hell, was someone trying to pick off the Reynolds family one by one? And for what reason?

"They both could died," Sandra said again. "First Adam and now Dahlia and Taylor. This entire family is in danger. We could all be killed in our sleep tonight."

"I'm not going to let anyone else be murdered," Eli replied firmly. "I've called in all my part-time deputies and even borrowed a few from the neighboring county that are looking for overtime. We're going to keep a close watch on everyone."

Taylor was still crying but Dahlia and Sandra appeared somewhat mollified. No one, however, looked happy. Least of all Eli.

A deputy jogged onto the patio then, holding what looked

like a shotgun wrapped in a handkerchief.

"Sheriff, we found this near the property line. It looks recently fired."

Eli accepted the firearm from the deputy, examining it from end to end. He held out the gun for Dahlia's inspection.

"There are initials on the handle. D and R. Is this your rifle, Dahlia?"

Her eyes widened and she shook her head. "It's not mine."

"I know who that belongs to," Taylor said, pointing to the gun. "It belongs to David. That's his. I've seen him use it when he goes hunting. David tried to kill us."

David? Honestly, it wasn't a far stretch. He'd already said some nasty things about his father. Would he try to kill his sister and niece too?

It looked like Eli and Jared needed to have a chat with David Reynolds.

CHAPTER FOURTEEN

This was certainly an interesting turn of events. Jared hadn't had the most fuzzy and warm feelings for David Reynolds from the beginning so he wasn't at all shocked that he might be a strong suspect in his father's death.

Currently, Eli had several deputies scouring the estate looking for the man but so far, he hadn't turned up. His vehicle was still in the garage though, so he should be on the property.

Jared, on the other hand, was sticking close to the house and keeping an eye on the residents. While they – including Misty – were all in the living room talking and comforting Taylor, he took the opportunity to call Jason, who had sent a text earlier that he had some information.

"How's it going down there?" Jason asked when he picked up the phone. "Any closer to finding the killer?"

"Maybe," Jared replied. "Someone took a couple of shots at Dahlia and her daughter Taylor while they were out riding. One of their deputies found a rifle with David Reynolds' initials on it. They're looking for him now."

"They shot at them?"

"According to Dahlia, she heard three shots and then her

horse bolted."

"Three shots?"

"You keep repeating everything I'm saying."

Jason chuckled. "You're right, I am. I'm just trying to picture the scene. The two of them were riding and someone was waiting for them, presumably in a location that would allow them to see and be close enough to their victims to shoot them but not be seen. Then they shot three times, missed all three times and then disappeared, leaving the firearm behind. That doesn't bother you in any way?"

Frankly, Jared hadn't had time to think about the scenario but now that his friend had pointed it out...

It did seem a little weird.

"I guess the person could be a lousy shot."

"They could," Jason conceded. "Or maybe they weren't trying to kill anyone. They might have been trying to scare them. I don't know that for sure but it's something to think about."

"I'll be thinking about it." Jared rubbed at the back of his neck where the muscles were tightening up painfully with stress. "I hope you have better news for me than I had for you."

"I definitely have news but I don't know if it's good or bad. We've been elbow deep researching the Reynolds family since you called. It's all hands on deck here so we can get you back as soon as possible."

"Tell everyone that dinner is on me when we get back. I'm grateful."

"I'll tell them you'll buy them a juicy steak. Now I'll go over the information with you on the phone, but then I'll send the detailed research to your email."

"I'll keep an eye out for it."

"First, I found out there were some rumors that Adam Reynolds was thinking of selling Chipper Shopper. They started a few months ago, I'm assuming right after his diagnosis. Whether he was actually in any talks or negotiations I don't know. Certainly, he would have had interest if he wanted to sell."

"He didn't say anything about it when we talked to him," Jared said. "But then we didn't really talk business with him. He and Misty mostly talked about her mother, and she told him about her childhood. What else did you find out?"

"We'll start with his ex-wife Sandra. From what I was able to dig up, her husband pretty much cheated on her constantly. He had a year-long affair with Sandra's best friend and he's had NDA agreements with several women that worked for him. Apparently, Sandra mostly turned a blind eye in the beginning, but when the kids got older she eventually filed for divorce. They didn't have a prenup so she received a generous settlement. But to get that settlement she had to give up something. She gave up primary custody of the kids. He got that. Instead, she got every other weekend, two months in the summer, and a week at Christmas. That's it."

"That's…strange. He pushed her out of her own children's lives. That's fucked up."

Adam Reynolds was a real piece of work and this only made the billionaire even more of an asshole in Jared's eyes.

"Exactly, and from what I could find Reynolds wasn't an involved parent. The kids were mostly raised by a series of nannies and babysitters. Eventually, Sandra moved closer to Adam when the kids were in their late teens and they all decided to try and be one big happy divorced family. As for what Sandra did before that, she traveled a great deal, mostly in Europe."

"So Sandra had motive. Revenge for sending her away while the kids grew up."

"Sadly, she's not the only one," Jason said grimly. "She's just the tip of the iceberg. David Reynolds wasn't fond of his father, either."

"And he's vocal about it too," Jared agreed. "He'd barely met me and he told me how much he hated this house and his dad."

"He has good reason to. David wanted to go to art school but his dad wouldn't let him. He forced his son to go to an Ivy League university and major in business. David wouldn't have gotten in without dear old dad greasing the wheels for him, either. His grades were mediocre and he didn't have much in the way of extracurriculars. Yet somehow, he managed entrance into one of the most exclusive schools in the country."

"While in college," Jason went on, "David fell in love with another student and they planned to get married. Enter dear old dad. He decided that the female wasn't good enough for his son and paid the girl's mother off to convince her daughter that David was just playing with her affections. It's all kinds of fucked over."

"I would hate my dad too," Jared declared. "Jesus, Adam Reynolds was a bastard."

"It gets better. David finally graduates – barely – then starts working in the executive offices at Chipper Shopper just like daddy wants and then falls in love for a second time. His assistant. She gets pregnant, David proposes, and they head down to the courthouse to get married. This time he wasn't going to give his dad a chance to intervene, but it turns out he was too late. Reynolds literally had his son's office bugged for sound and knew the day they were headed to city hall. He had a couple of goons waiting for him and they kidnapped David and dragged him away. The stress for his fiancée was so bad she miscarried their child. Reynolds fired her and then sent David to work in London for a year."

"Holy fuck. It's amazing no one murdered Adam before

now."

"I agree. Now Dahlia is a different story. She never fought her dad about anything. She married the man that he picked out for her and that was that. Eventually they divorced but by then she'd produced an heir and Reynolds was happy. Here's the creepy part. Taylor's upbringing was controlled by Adam, not Dahlia. The private school he sent her to didn't even realize she had a mother until Dahlia showed up at the graduation ceremony. It looks like he's been grooming Taylor to take over his business empire."

"Which goes against the rumors that he was going to sell."

"That's all they were. Rumors. Could be right, could be wrong. It's still interesting. Maybe Taylor had started to rebel and he decided to sell rather than deal with persuading her to toe the line. Remember, he didn't have long left and he probably didn't want to spend it arguing with his granddaughter."

"She did seem close to her grandfather, but she also seems quite close to her mother as well. What else do you have for me?"

"Lydia and Tom. First, Lydia has been with Adam Reynolds for years. Decades. She started with the company fresh out of college and worked her way up to being Reynolds' personal assistant."

"Were they having an affair the whole time?" Jared asked.

"It's hard to say. She was married at one point for a few years, but they divorced. She moved in with Reynolds about five years ago. I'm told she was pushing for marriage, but he was adamant about staying single."

Jared couldn't see Lydia killing her significant other because he wouldn't marry her. It was a motive, but a weak one.

"And Tom? What's his story?"

"You're going to love this," Jason laughed. "He's married.

Two kids."

"Wait…he's *married*? But he was kissing Dahlia and Taylor."

Tom should be exhausted.

"Married. For about eight years. His wife and kids live in Monterey. He lives close to the Reynolds estate and goes home to visit about once a month. They rent a home, have two cars, one that's paid off, and they like to watch Netflix and order pizza on Saturday nights. They're saving to buy a house and Tom has been actively looking for a better-paying job with Chipper Shopper competitors which would be a huge issue. Tom has a non-compete clause in his employment contract. He's not allowed to work for a direct competitor for five years. I'm not sure how he was planning to pull that off. Maybe he was hoping that after Reynolds' death whoever took over wouldn't enforce it."

"I would never have guessed it. I wonder if anyone knows or perhaps Adam found out. It gives Tom motive but once again not necessarily a strong one."

"Reynolds has pissed off a bunch of people over the years, not surprisingly. Nothing that really stands out. People who have slipped and fell in his stores, employees that feel they weren't treated fairly. There is one lawsuit that is slightly more interesting. A builder suing for breach of contract. They're saying that Reynolds agreed to finance a fancy outdoor shopping mall and then backed out after signing the papers. Not much on this one. It's in the early stages of the lawsuit so there's not much information."

"A billionaire being sued over contracts? Not that groundbreaking," Jared observed. "I'd be more shocked if he wasn't being sued by his business partners. In fact, I'm surprised we only found the one."

"Me too," Jason agreed. "Although it only takes one slightly unhinged human being who feels they've been wronged. Was Reynolds receiving any threats before his death?"

"Not that I know of, but I'll double check with Eli."

"So tell me about this sheriff. Is he good? Do you think he can solve this case?"

Jared had given this question some thought.

"He seems like a good man, and yes, I think he can solve it without my help. I assume that was the unspoken part of your question."

"It was, but I know you. You're not going to just up and leave him. You'll make sure this is solved. Not just because you can't stand loose ends, but for Misty."

"She's having a tough time with this."

"I would imagine. She'll be fine, though. She's a strong woman, and she has you, plus family and friends. As soon as you guys get home, we'll all go out for dinner. Brinley was mentioning that the other day."

"We'll do that," Jared promised. "We've been homebodies quite a bit lately. Getting out and about would do us both good."

"Good luck and call me if you need anything."

Jared promised he would and they ended their call. He was glad that his friends were able to find out information regarding the Reynolds family, but it didn't really help all that much. Every single one of them was a suspect before and now...they were still suspects. It hasn't ruled out anyone. He and Eli needed another round of questioning.

They'd start with David and his recently fired gun.

CHAPTER FIFTEEN

"I didn't do anything," David moaned, holding his head in his hands. He was sitting in the kitchen drinking coffee to try and sober up from another bender. "I've been sleeping for the last two hours."

Sleeping was another word for passed out, apparently. This time they'd found him asleep in the utility shed among the clay pots and fertilizer.

"Is this your rifle?" Eli asked, holding out the firearm. "Please be sure before answering."

"It's mine. Those are my initials. But I didn't fire at anyone. I haven't used that gun in months."

"Where do you store your firearms, David?" Jared asked. "Are they accessible to anyone else?"

"They're stored in the hallway off the mud and laundry room. There's a cabinet there with the family firearms."

Eli scribbled in his notebook. "Is it locked?"

"Yes, but the key is hanging up by the back door." David pointed to a row of keys, each one hanging by a small hook on the wall. "Anyone in the house could have unlocked it."

That made little to no sense to Jared.

"Then why bother to lock them up?"

"I dunno. That's how we've always done it." David took another gulp of black coffee. "Listen, I wouldn't hurt my sister or my niece. I love them, they're my family. I would never do that."

"Did anyone see you go into the garage?" Eli queried. "Can anyone confirm your whereabouts this afternoon?"

Scraping a hand through his hair, David shrugged. "I'm not sure. I grabbed a bottle of whiskey from the pantry after lunch and then went for a walk. I guess I ended up in the garage. I don't know how I got there. Everything after lunch is a blur."

Eli sighed and shook his head. "Do you black out regularly?"

"Sometimes."

Jared could barely hear David's reply since he'd whispered it, his head down in shame. Jesus, Mary, and Joseph this was pathetic.

"You need to seek help," Eli said firmly. "Professional help, and probably a month or two in a quality rehab. You're drinking is so out of control you have no idea whether you tried to kill your own family."

David's head shot up. "I know I didn't do that. I love my family."

"You didn't love your father," Jared pointed out. "You hated him."

"I hated this house and I hated the way my father treated me, but I loved him. I wouldn't have hurt him. Ever."

Jared's gut was telling him that this man was telling the truth, but he needed to push him a little bit. He needed to be *sure*.

"You didn't hate him when he wouldn't let you go to art school? And you didn't hate him when he broke up your relationship and paid her mother off? You're a better man than I am, David, because I would have been pretty pissed off. Then

Adam had the nerve to do it again, trying to get you to toe the family line. He kidnapped you from your own wedding ceremony. That didn't make you madder than hell? I guess you got a free trip to London out of it."

The other man's face went pale and a muscle jumped in his jaw. "You don't know what you're talking about."

"Are you sure? It sounds like your dad was a controlling son of a bitch to me. No one would blame you if you were mad."

"I was not mad."

"Then you're a saint."

"I was not mad."

This time David said it louder, his lips trembling with emotion that he was clearly trying to suppress.

Eli knelt down next to David's chair so they were eye to eye. "Did you kill your father, David? It's okay. We understand. Maybe you two fought and it got heated. It was an accident, right? Accidents happen all of the time."

David shook his head over and over, his eyes bright with unshed tears. "No, no, no. I didn't kill him. I wouldn't do that."

"You'd been drinking," Eli said. "You were upset. You told me you went to get the bottle of rum and you went to drink outside. What happened after that?"

"I don't remember."

"Did you go talk to your father? Did you argue with him?"

"No, I didn't see him after dinner. I went and got drunk." David looked up at Jared, his expression heartbroken as more tears slipped down his cheeks. "I didn't kill him. I know that I didn't. I loved my father, and I hated him too. But not enough to hurt him. All I wanted him to do was to leave me alone. I just wanted to be alone."

Eli stood and pulled Jared aside. "I don't know whether to believe him or not. I'm leaning toward I do."

"He seems sincere, but I think it's more that he doesn't even remember what he's done most of his waking hours. The guy has a huge drinking problem. As out of it as he was last night, I can't imagine him having the physical dexterity to come up behind Adam and hit him over the head. He could barely walk. As for shooting that rifle, maybe. He didn't hit anything which kind of goes with being drunk. Let forensics try to lift some fingerprints – other than his – from that firearm."

"You think someone could be trying to frame him? His own damn family?"

"This family is a viper pit. I wouldn't turn my back on any of them. I'd be afraid of getting a knife in my back."

Eli chuckled in understanding. "I don't blame you. So where does that leave us?"

"About where we were before, although I do have a lot to tell you. My firm dug up some interesting information about this family. Spoiler alert. None of it is good."

"I had a feeling that you knew some things I didn't when you talked to David about his dad breaking up his wedding. Christ, did Adam really do that?"

"He did. Remember what I said...viper pit."

"Maybe if we just lock them all in a room, they'll destroy each other and leave the rest of society out of it."

That wasn't a bad idea. Except...

There would still be one left at the end.

"Did Jared tell you to call me?"

Misty's husband thought he was being so sneaky but she had his number. She and his brother Ty were close – like siblings – but he wouldn't call in the middle of their weekend out of town unless it was an emergency. Or Jared had asked him to.

She'd retreated to a side porch that she'd discovered when exploring the house. It didn't look used that often, but it was comfortable with a wicker sofa and a few chairs along with a small round table. Mostly, it was quiet.

"Why do you say that? Can't I just call my favorite sister-in-law?"

"I'm your only sister-in-law."

"For now. It looks like Royce is going to propose any day now. He and Anna are getting serious."

Misty liked Anna a great deal and Royce was lucky to have found a woman that could deal with his checkered past and look toward their own future.

"I hope she says yes."

"I think she will."

"But that's not the reason you called. You called because Jared asked you to."

There was a heavy sigh on the other end of the line. "Fine, he asked me to but of course I said yes. I adore you and I love talking to you. This isn't a burden."

"He's worried about me."

"Jared was born worried," Ty laughed. "I swear he's had a concerned expression on his face since he was three years old. You've seen the pictures of when he was a kid. He was an old man before he hit puberty. He worried about his mortgage and car payment before he even had a house and a car."

"And you don't worry at all?"

"I worry just enough, although Kyle thinks that I worry far too much. I think worrying runs in the Monroe DNA. Speaking of worrying, I was actually glad that Jared wanted me to call you. I'm worried about him."

"Why? He's been stressed about the business growing so quickly and Nate's been acting up in school, but mostly we've been okay."

Then Misty remembered that Jared was already worried about Lizzie and boys and dating and all that entailed. She'd assured him that it was all going to be fine but perhaps he'd talked to Ty about it.

"It's not the business or the kids, Mist. It's Dad, or should I say Dad's death. He doesn't want to talk about it or deal with it. I'm worried that he's in some weird state of denial. Does he talk about it with you?"

"A little," she admitted. "When I bring it up, but not voluntarily."

"And he seems just fine, I assume," Ty replied. "He always does. He allowed himself to grieve at the funeral but then right after he snapped back into Jared Monroe-super cop mode. I have a bad feeling that he's going to hit a wall eventually and not know how to deal with all of his emotions. I know that he has you there but shit, now you're dealing with your own issues with your dad."

Honestly, Misty hadn't even yet begun to deal with those issues. It was going to take time to process all the crap she'd been through since that letter arrived.

"I'm okay for now. It's going to be a process to deal with this. But I hear what you're saying about Jared. He hasn't really wanted to talk about Gerald, and I haven't wanted to push. He does everything in his own time."

"He does," Ty agreed. "I just don't want it to hit him out of the blue. For a man as intelligent as my brother, he can be strangely naive about his own inner workings and emotions."

That was Jared in a nutshell. Devastatingly smart, but not about himself. He had to be hit over the head with the truth from time to time.

"I'll talk to him when we get back home. I doubt he'll open

up to me while we're here. He's already suspicious and on edge. He doesn't like the Reynolds family and he hasn't held back in telling me so."

"What about you? Do you like your new family?"

Did she? She wasn't sure that she did. She was trying to be open-minded, though.

"I don't think I'd call them my family. When we leave here I may never see these people again, to be honest."

"If they're anything like my brother described, it might be for the best."

The Reynolds family definitely had issues. Lots of them.

Was one of them a murderer? Hopefully, Eli and Jared would find out. In the meantime, she was determined to keep her distance as much as possible. She wanted Adam's killer to be found.

Then she wanted to go home.

CHAPTER SIXTEEN

The last thing Jared and Misty wanted to do was sit down with the family for dinner. It was already tense and neither of them thought it would improve once everyone sat down at the same table to eat.

David had been sent upstairs to sleep off his hangover after being told by Eli that they'd talk again later when he was more alert. Dahlia and Taylor were swearing up and down they were going to leave the house because they couldn't stay under the same roof as a possible murderer. Eli hadn't told them to stay, and in fact had encouraged them to move to the same hotel that Jared and Misty had planned to stay in a few towns over, but so far they liked complaining more than actually leaving.

Taylor's boyfriend Brent had shown up at one point and declared he was going to take her back to his house. That hadn't happened either. Instead, Brent and Taylor had invited their friends over and they were hanging out on the back patio.

Eli wanted to talk to Tom after learning that the assistant had been keeping a few secrets so he, Jared, and Misty had driven into town together. Tom was renting a small condo there.

They dropped Misty off at the local cafe, which was pretty

much the only place open past six in the evening while they headed to Tom's. They'd join her later for dinner but in the meantime, she could relax out of the Reynolds place, have a few cups of coffee, and read a good book. Eli assured them that she'd be welcome and even introduced them to the owner of the place.

"So what's the plan?" Eli asked Jared as they exited the sheriff's SUV. "Good cop/bad cop or two bad cops?"

Chuckling, Jared shook his head. "With guys like David Reynolds you play the good cop, the friend just trying to help out. With a guy like Tom Butler? I'd go in and scare the living shit out of him. A slick professional who thinks that he can fool everyone, all the time. He needs to learn that there's no such thing as a safe secret."

"Sounds like a plan. I called him so he's expecting us."

They didn't even have to ring the doorbell. The door flew open the minute they set foot on the front porch. Butler had been watching for them at the window, apparently. Was he nervous?

He looked nervous. He was all smiles and welcome, but Jared could see the slight tremble in the other man's hands and the false brightness in his expression. Tom Butler was concerned about their visit.

"Can I get you anything?" Butler offered. "Coffee? Water? A beer?"

"I'm fine," Jared replied, taking in the surroundings. If he hadn't known Butler lived here, he wouldn't have been able to guess. It looked like a generic hotel room, but then the guy had a family home elsewhere.

"I'm good," Eli said. "How about we all sit down and have a chat?"

Butler swallowed hard, his Adam's apple bobbing up and

down. "Is that what this is? A chat? I have to admit that I'm wondering why you need to talk to me again. I've already given a statement."

The man sounded so hopeful. But a little scared, too. Jared almost felt sorry for him.

Almost, but not quite.

"We have a few other questions," Eli replied as they settled on the couch. Jared sat next to him and Butler sat across from them in an overstuffed chair. "First of all, is there anything else that you'd like to tell us, Tom? Anything at all that you may have left out of your statement?"

Butler looked down at the floor and then back up. "I don't think so. Why do you ask?"

Eli glanced at Jared before continuing. "Jared has been doing some research to help us with this case. It's come to our attention that you've been looking for a new job, specifically with Chipper Shopper competitors."

The blood drained from Butler's face and then returned quickly, only this time bright red.

"I–I don't know what you're talking about. That's not true."

Jared pulled his notes from his breast pocket and unfolded them, scanning the page for the exact part that he wanted.

"So you didn't travel to Indianapolis three weeks ago to speak to the Marketing Director of Shopper's Nirvana? That wasn't you?"

Licking his lips, Butler squirmed in his chair. "Well...yes. That was me but it's not what you're thinking. They called me. They were headhunting me. I wasn't looking to make a change."

"Then Vendor's Square was also headhunting you?" Jared asked. "Because you traveled to their headquarters in Texas ten days ago."

Another bob of Butler's Adam's apple. "Uh...well...yeah.

They were headhunting me."

The guy was lying out of his ass and it was obvious. Jared's rookie deputies would have been able to see through this bullshit.

"So even though you weren't looking to make any change of employment you went on at least two different interviews?"

"Listen, I loved working for Adam," Tom said, hopping up from his chair. "He was practically a father to me."

Butler had opened the door…

"Was Dahlia like a sister to you then? Because we saw you kissing her outside by the pool the night Adam was murdered."

"That isn't how it looked."

Now Butler was pacing the small space and visibly sweating, his forehead shiny. Panicked as all hell. This wasn't going to get any better for him, though.

"I'm sure you can explain it," Jared said. "You might also want to explain kissing Taylor that night as well. She's barely legal. How long has that been going on? And one more question. Does your wife know about any of this?"

Butler stopped pacing abruptly, his skin now pasty white. He opened his mouth several times to answer but no sound came out except a few squeaks. He took a step forward but then his eyes seemed to roll back and he began to fall toward the floor. Jared and Eli had to leap up to catch him before he hit his head on the coffee table between them.

Tom Butler had fainted during his questioning.

"More iced tea?" the cafe waitress asked Misty. "Do you want something to munch on while you wait for your husband? I can get Ken to whip you up some fries or bring out some fresh bread."

The fresh bread sounded delicious. Misty had smelled the aroma wafting from other tables, making her stomach growl with hunger. She'd been trying to hold out for Jared and Eli to get back, but her tummy had other ideas.

"The bread sounds wonderful, thank you," Misty said. "They should be here soon, I hope."

The waitress' gaze ran around the half-empty room. "We're not busy tonight. You're fine to sit here all night if you want. My name's Robin, by the way. If you need anything just call or wave me down."

"Thank you, Robin."

The friendly waitress was probably in her mid-twenties. Slim and pretty, she seemed to know all of the customers, addressing them by their first names. She was only gone a few minutes before reappearing with a basket of warm bread.

"Are you enjoying your stay at the Reynolds' estate?"

"How did you know we were staying there?" Misty asked, taking a sip of her iced tea.

Robin laughed and waved her pencil around the cafe. "There are no secrets in this little town. Everybody knows everything about everybody. There's no need to print a newspaper because we'd all know what was going on before it was ever delivered to your doorstep."

"I come from one of those towns, too," Misty sighed. "Ever heard of Fielding, Montana?"

"Can't say that I have."

"No one has."

Robin tucked the menus she was carrying under her arm. "You gotta love a small town. Gossip travels at the speed of light, and that Reynolds family sure keeps chins wagging around here. I don't know what we did for entertainment until they moved in about twenty years ago."

"I sort of assumed Adam grew up around here."

"No, I think he's from the Eureka area," Robin replied with a shake of her head. "My mom always talks about how he came in like a whirlwind and bought up a bunch of land and then built that fancy house on it. Most folks around here don't have that kind of money so it was quite an event."

"It is a lovely piece of land."

Misty wasn't as enamored of the house. Too big and too fussy for her taste.

"So I'll be honest with you. Everyone in town is talking about you and your husband. Whether you're a family friend or a business partner."

In other words, Robin wanted to get the scoop as to Misty and Jared's identity. At this point, it was all up in the air.

"We're new friends, I guess you could say. Adam knew some of my family years ago before I was born."

Robin nodded in understanding. "So you met them recently? They're an interesting bunch for sure. Especially the granddaughter Taylor. She's a wild one."

Taylor? Wild? That didn't go with the image that Adam had painted. Misty would have expected that Taylor was studious and ambitious.

"How is she wild? She still manages to get good grades. Adam said she's going to Stanford in the fall."

"She's a smart one, there's no doubt. She went to a private school near San Francisco. Got good grades. But when she came home for vacations or break, she and her boyfriend Brent would run wild through this town. Drinking and partying in the woods, bullying kids they don't like, and just generally being juvenile delinquents. Do they even use that word anymore? If not, they should. I think she does it to get her mother's attention, but Dahlia Reynolds isn't really the motherly type, if you know what

I mean. She does nothing to control Taylor and honestly spends most of her time in New York City with her latest boyfriend."

"Dahlia doesn't spend any time here?"

Misty had been under the impression that she lived at the house, but then she'd never actually asked who were residents and who might just be visiting besides Sandra.

"She comes around once in awhile, but I never got the idea that she liked it. To be honest, I think only the old man liked it out here. His ex-wife didn't and his mistress Lydia sure as hell doesn't. She's too good to even step into this place. Walks around with her nose in the air. Don't know what she has to be so high and mighty about. Everyone knows that the old man was never going to marry her. She knew it too. Everyone around town has always said that he was still seeing his ex-wife all these years. Plenty of other women too. She was just one of them."

Adam had been honest about his infidelities, and leopards rarely changed their spots. He probably had been unfaithful to Lydia as well as Sandra.

"You seem to know a lot of the Reynolds family," Misty observed. Some of this might be useful as Jared and Eli searched for Adam's killer. "What else do you know?"

Robin shrugged. "Like I said, they're a real interesting family. They don't seem to like each other much so none of us were really surprised that the old man ended up dead the way he did. He was a nice man, though. He tipped big whenever he came in. The son is a big tipper too. He's seeing a nice woman in the next town over. I think they're getting serious."

David had a girlfriend? Had Adam found out?

Just ask her. Go ahead.

"You said that you're not surprised. Who do you think killed Adam Reynolds?"

There. She'd asked it.

Robin's brows rose at the question and a smile played around her lips. "You want to know who I think killed the old man? There's been a bunch of talk about that these last few days. I'll tell you who I think the murderer is, and I'll tell you why. Dahlia Reynolds. I've never seen a colder woman in my entire life. She doesn't care about anyone but herself. From what I hear, she's been planning to take over the family business for years and cut out her own brother."

"You think she killed her own father?"

"I do," Robin confirmed. "She's been eyeing the prize for years. Maybe she got tired of waiting or maybe the old man was planning to give it all to his son. Who knows the reasons? But I definitely think she was capable."

The bell over the door jangled and Jared and Eli walked in.

"Looks like Eli and your husband are here. I'll leave these menus and come back in a few minutes to get your orders."

Placing the menus on the table, Robin disappeared into the kitchen. Jared sat next to Misty and Eli sat opposite.

"Did Robin fill you in on all the town gossip?" Eli asked with a teasing grin. "This town loves to talk."

"She did. I didn't realize that David had a local girlfriend. Do you think that Adam knew about her?"

"I'd heard the rumors but I don't have any confirmation on whether that story is true," Eli replied. "I did ask David when I talked to him about his girlfriend, but he said she doesn't exist. That's all we have right now...gossip. They get it wrong as much as they get it right."

"She also thinks that Dahlia did it."

"She could have," Jared said, opening his menu. "So could have several other people. At this point, we just don't know. Adam Reynolds wasn't a well-liked guy."

Too many suspects, too many motives. Misty had no doubt

that Jared and Eli would eventually solve the mystery. Meanwhile there was another question that still remained unanswered.

Was Adam her biological father?

CHAPTER SEVENTEEN

When Jared and Misty had returned to the house the night before they'd been greeted by Lydia, who had informed them that the memorial service was being held the next afternoon. They'd specifically scheduled it that way so Misty could attend.

It would be a small, private affair at the local church with just family and a few friends. The reading of the will would be held at the house right after.

There was no graceful way to get out of attending, and it was clear that Misty wanted to go so Jared had pasted a smile on his face and thanked the older woman for being so accommodating.

"You're not hiding your irritation very well," Misty teased him that morning as she helped him with his tie. She looked lovely in the one dress she'd brought, a dark blue number that brought out the color in her eyes. "You'll have to do better at the service."

"I'm not irritated."

He sounded it though.

"You are most certainly irritated, my handsome husband. You don't want to go today."

He didn't know how to put his feelings into words. Whenever he thought about what to say he inwardly winced. He sounded like a judgmental jerk.

"Let's just say that there are places I'd rather be, but nothing is going to keep me from being there to support you today. I love you and I know this means a lot to you."

She stopped fiddling with his tie and let her warm palms rest on his chest. "He might be my father. I know in my head that he wasn't necessarily a good person, but my heart is currently running the show."

Jared ran his fingertip across her jaw, enjoying the satin of her soft skin. "I think your heart is one of the most beautiful things about you. I love that you can see past all the crap that I hold onto. Your ability to see the best in people is amazing. Thank god you see the good in me, honey."

"There's more than a bit there."

"Sometimes I wonder. I think I'm getting damn cynical in my old age."

"Considering what you do for a living that's not a huge shock. You see the worst of humanity on a regular basis."

"No excuse. I know that there's goodness in this world, but I don't spend near enough time thinking about it as I do the assholes."

"That's because the assholes are louder and demand more attention."

Jared leaned down and brushed her lips with his own, wishing that they weren't due somewhere soon. He made a mental note to plan a second honeymoon for the two of them. The kids were old enough now that they enjoyed a few days away from their parents.

"True. Are you ready to go? I need to stop for gas on the way to the church."

They headed down to the garage that was near the house. It was more of a warehouse really, filled with dozens of vehicles, most of them incredibly expensive or rare. Sometimes both.

Jared's SUV looked quite utilitarian next to the sexy sports models and vintage automobiles. Misty paused next to a Bentley, taking in the graceful lines of the vehicle.

"This looks expensive."

Chuckling, Jared hit the unlock button on his key fob. "It is. That car starts at about two hundred thousand and goes from there."

She took a few steps back. "Then I don't want to touch it. I'm afraid I might scratch it."

He didn't have a chance to respond, however, as the lights in the garage went out. There was the sound of a car engine firing up, then another, and then another, one right after the other. The massive overhead garage doors hadn't opened though. Someone had started the cars remotely.

"Stay here," Jared commanded. "I'm going to try and open the garage door."

There was just enough light seeping through the doors that he was able to make his way to the console of buttons on the wall. He pressed one and then another, but nothing budged. He'd been hoping for a battery or generator backup. If he'd been able to open the large doors, fresh air would instantly rush into the oversized room.

No such luck. They'd go out the way they'd come in. If he couldn't get his car out, no one could which would mean they would all be late for the memorial service.

He waved to Misty to go to the side door. "We'll just go out that way. We'll have to get our car later."

When he tried the door, however, it didn't move either. It was locked. Had it locked automatically when the power went out? Adam had to have some sort of security for all of these expensive vehicles.

Or...and this was where he was leaning...had someone locked the door on purpose? Trapping himself and Misty inside a garage while three cars pumped out deadly carbon dioxide. His gut was telling him that he didn't have time to ponder the question. He needed to get them out of there. Right the hell now. He'd worry about the why and the who later.

"Jared?"

Misty sounded scared. She'd already figured out for herself that this situation wasn't good. He didn't need to go into any detail and frankly, he didn't have the time.

"I'm going to get us out of here."

If it was the last fucking thing he'd ever do.

Then he'd kill the bastard that had done this.

Someone had killed Adam and was now trying to kill herself and Jared. Misty didn't have time to contemplate why a person would do that. She'd save that for later. Right now they had to figure a way out of here before they both passed out and died.

"Stay right here," Jared commanded. "I'm going to try and turn off those cars."

"You'll never figure out which ones are running in time," Misty said, grabbing his arm and pulling him back. "It's too dark in here and there are too many of them."

There were at least thirty cars in that garage in four rows and they'd heard three engines start up.

"Shit. Okay, then I'm going to find a tool to break that lock."

On the back wall of the garage there were drawers and cabinets filled with tools and supplies to work on the vehicles. Surely there had to be something there that could open the door. This was not how Misty wanted to go out. She wanted to see her kids again. She didn't want to die in a damn garage.

Jared jogged through the dark and she could hear the opening and closing of drawers and cabinets. She shined her flashlight toward him and then she could see him running back, a large crowbar and a hammer in his hand.

"I'll try the crowbar first. Step back a little, honey."

The room was beginning to spin and she felt woozy, her knees weak. She had to grab onto the wall to steady herself.

Grunting, Jared dug the crowbar into the space between the door and the frame, pushing at the handle until she heard some sort of a snap and then the door flew open. A rush of fresh air filled her lungs as Jared dragged her outside, both of them falling onto the ground. She clung to him as the sounds of footsteps filled her ears, and then Eli was there. She could hear him asking Jared what happened and then her husband's voice answering but it all sounded so far away, like they were in a tunnel or something.

"Misty, open your eyes," Jared commanded, giving her a little shake. "Take some deep breaths. Come on, you can do it."

She didn't want to, her lungs hurt, but she did it anyway, the increase in oxygen causing the earth to undulate underneath her but then it settled down. She was able to sit on the ground without it moving.

"Misty, talk to me," Eli said. "What are the names of your kids?"

"Lizzie and Nate and I'm fine," she said, holding her head so everything would stay still. "Just dizzy. We were locked in."

"You certainly were. I'm just glad I was still here," he said with a long sigh. "Thank goodness you two knew what to do. The carbon monoxide from three cars would have done you in."

"I think that was the whole point," Jared said, his voice gravelly. "Someone tried to kill us."

"They almost succeeded," Eli replied, a grim tone in his voice. "A few more minutes and it would have been too late."

First Adam, then Dahlia and Taylor, and now Jared and herself. What did this killer want? Why them?

They needed to find out who was doing this before they killed someone else.

Jared had left Misty up in their bedroom resting while he and Eli surveyed the area around the warehouse for any clues. They walked the entire perimeter looking for footprints or maybe something small left behind but came up with nothing. Eli had already called the forensics team – again – and they were going to come out and dust the door and the circuit breaker panel for fingerprints.

In the meantime, Jared's anger had built until he wanted to put his fist through a wall. Or maybe the killer's face. When he thought about how Misty had looked when he'd dragged her out of that poisoned garage…

He was furious with himself that he'd allowed a murderer to get that close to her. He should have been more careful.

"Jared, are you listening to me?"

"Of course I am," Jared snapped back. "You were talking about the goddamn door."

"Actually, I was talking about the distance a human being could be standing from the garage and still remotely start those cars."

"Too far. They could do it from inside the house. That's the whole damn point of starting a car remotely."

Eli turned and stared at the mansion. "I can't believe that all these people around here didn't see anything."

"They're too focused on themselves. I've never seen such a narcissistic bunch. I just want to get Misty out of here."

"I know you're blaming yourself," Eli said. "I know you're pissed off, but I need you to channel that anger in a productive manner. We have a killer to catch."

Jared wasn't the most patient of men and he'd just about reached the end of his rope.

"Heaven help the asshole when we do catch him. If anything had happened to Misty—"

"Nothing did," Eli interjected. "You handled everything perfectly. You're both alright."

"This time."

"I won't let anything happen to you."

Jared shook his head. "You can't promise that and I would never ask you to. I'm taking Misty home first thing in the morning. She's safer far away from here."

"And the killer?"

"I trust that you'll catch him or her. But I can't wait around to have them try again. They've already tried to kill Dahlia and Taylor."

"You think it's a warning?"

"I don't know." Eli grimaced and shook his head. "The one thing we know for sure is that the killer is still hanging around here. If I had killed someone, I sure as shit wouldn't hang around the crime scene and draw attention to myself. Would you?"

No, he wouldn't which made this all the more…fascinating. Nothing was making sense.

"I don't think this is a hitman," Jared finally replied. "This is definitely an amateur."

"Which means we'll find him. Or her. Eventually, they're

going to do something really stupid."

"And that's why I trust that you'll find the person."

If Jared had his way, he'd bundle his wife up in the car and take her home immediately. He knew that wouldn't fly, however. She wanted to go to the memorial service and pay her respects. So they'd do that. Then tomorrow morning he'd take her home.

No one was going to get anywhere near Misty. Not again.

CHAPTER EIGHTEEN

"**Y**ou could have died."

Misty didn't need her best friend Rayne telling her the obvious. She'd already heard it from Jared, then Sandra, then the EMT who had arrived at the estate in an ambulance. Then Lydia and Dahlia had said it again when they'd come outside to find out why there was an ambulance on the property.

Thankfully, Jared and Misty hadn't needed to go to the hospital but so far everyone had said the same thing.

You could have died.

"I didn't die though, so let's not dwell on it too much."

Although it had been scary as hell sitting on the grass with an oxygen mask over her face. She didn't want a repeat of that ever again.

"Jared must be livid."

"Well…yes. He's not happy that they got this close. He keeps saying he should have known, but of course, there's no way he should have known the person would come after us."

Jared and Eli were currently stomping around downstairs and growling at everyone that dared cross their path. They were checking for footprints outside the garage and interrogating every member of the household about what they might have seen or heard.

"So why would they go after you? Does this make it harder or easier to find your dad's killer?"

That was a good question. So far it hadn't made it any easier but when Misty thought about it…it should. Who had opportunity both times? Sort of like a Venn diagram intersecting.

"I have no idea why anyone would try and kill us. It doesn't make any sense. We barely know these people, and in a few days we'd be out of their lives forever."

"Would you really?" Rayne asked. "I hate to be the kind of person that brings this sort of stuff up but…maybe they think that your father left you something in his will and they don't like that. You've already said that they seem like a strange bunch. Perhaps they killed Adam for hate and money and tried to kill you for money too."

"I seriously doubt I'm in the will," Misty protested. "I just met Adam. We don't even know if he's truly my father. He just thinks he is. I don't have the DNA test back yet."

"Then maybe they just think you're a threat. If that DNA test comes back positive, they might think that you'll sue the estate for your share of the inheritance."

"I would never do that in a million years."

"But like you said, they don't know you. They don't know what you'd do so they see you as an impediment."

"You make it sound so cold-blooded."

"Because *it is cold-blooded*," Rayne said dryly. "They probably don't realize that the Monroe family has plenty of their own assets. You went there to find a family, not money. It looks like you're definitely not going to get the family that you hoped for. I'm sorry, Mist. This sucks all around."

"I'm fine," Misty assured Rayne. "I knew coming here that I

wasn't going to get some Hollywood happy ending. That was never in the cards."

"Aww, honey, I know you. You kind of wanted it, and damn, I'm sorry that you didn't get it. Life just hasn't been fair to you in the parental department."

True, but…

"I overachieved in marriage and children," Misty joked awkwardly. "Jared and the kids are better than I could have ever hoped."

"And I'm the sister you never had. And probably never wanted. Few people could get that lucky."

"You know I adore you," Misty giggled. "I couldn't have made it through all of this without you. You are my sister. I chose you so you're stuck with me."

"Stuck together for life. I can deal with that. Now when are you going home? I'm worried about you, Mist. I don't like the idea of you being somewhere with killers roaming freely."

Misty wasn't that thrilled about the situation either.

"Soon. I promise I won't end up dead."

"You better not. A shitty family is not worth getting killed for."

Words to live by.

But first…they needed to figure out who killed Adam and tried to kill her. And why did they do it?

Was it David who hated his father?

Sandra who divorced Adam?

Lydia who wanted to get married but Adam wouldn't?

Or was it Dahlia trying to protect her inheritance from Misty?

Or maybe Tom for an unknown reason?

They all had secrets.

Clearly some were more deadly than others.

✧ ✧ ✧ ✧

The mood was decidedly somber as Misty, Jared, and the rest of the family gathered in the living room after the memorial. The service hadn't been long. Dahlia had stood up and spoke a few words about what a wonderful father Adam was, and Lydia had talked about the businessman side of him. There had been a montage of photos and Misty had found that part fascinating, seeing all the images from so long ago. She could certainly see why her mother would have found him attractive. He'd been good-looking as a younger man.

David had sat off to the side, looking hungover and sad. Sandra sat next to Taylor and her boyfriend Brent, comforting the teenager when she cried. Tom was also there but he kept quite a distance between himself and everyone else, sitting in the back of the chapel. Eli had spoken briefly to him, but Misty hadn't overheard what was said.

A clergyman then led a short prayer and they were done. With no one saying a word, they'd all left the chapel and returned to the house where they would – in about an hour – receive guests from the nearby communities that wanted to pay their respects. In the meantime, the attorney had arrived to read the will.

It had all felt so final. Walking out of that chapel, Misty couldn't help but think that if Adam Reynolds was truly her biological father, she was never going to get a chance to really get to know him. She'd only have that conversation in his library that first day. That was it. She didn't even know if he liked chocolate ice cream. But most people like chocolate ice cream. Right?

If he'd held off sending that letter even a few weeks, this wouldn't have happened. She wouldn't have come here to meet him and she wouldn't be feeling so sad. Not just about his death, but about the missed opportunity. She could have gone on living her life the way she had been, content in not knowing who or what her father was. She'd made peace with that fact but now she had to find a way to find that peace again with a completely different set of circumstances. It was going to take time.

"Jared and I will go upstairs until the guests arrive," Misty said to Lydia. "We'll stay out of your way while the lawyer is here."

Lydia smiled and patted Misty's arm lightly. "You're so thoughtful, dear. Hopefully, it won't take long. It should be fairly straightforward. I'll send someone up to your room when we're done. I'll be helping the staff set up the food on the patio."

Misty and Jared had barely set foot on the bottom stair when Tom ran after them, calling their names.

"Wait," he said. "The attorney has requested that Misty be present as well."

"What on earth?" she muttered under breath. She had a very bad feeling about this.

"Your guess is as good as mine," Jared replied softly. "Looks like you've been summoned."

"You're going with me."

"I wouldn't miss this for the world."

She linked her arm with her husband's. "I don't have a good feeling. I shouldn't need to be in on this."

"I have that same feeling. Let's hope we're both wrong."

Maximillian Sharp had been Adam Reynolds' attorney for over thirty years. With gray hair and craggy features, he was dressed in a dark three-piece suit with an old-fashioned pocket watch in the vest. He certainly looked the part of a lawyer about to read a will, right down to the wire-rimmed glasses perched on his nose. He was sitting in a chair brought in from the dining room, his papers spread out on an end table.

The rest of the family had gathered in the living room, leaving a chair vacant for Misty near the empty fireplace. Jared perched on the arm and placed a reassuring hand on her shoulder. Her own hands were digging into the cushions as butterflies buzzed in her abdomen. She nervously licked her lips and ran her gaze around the room. Everyone but Max was looking at her, wondering why she was here.

I'm wondering too. Honestly, I'd rather not be present for this.

Clearing his throat, Max shuffled a few papers on his lap. "I think we're all here now so we can get started."

Taylor's eyes shot daggers at Misty, her lips pressed together in a thin line. "Why is *she* here?"

Max cleared his throat again. "Everyone is here for a reason. Now if we could get started, please?"

Sandra wrapped an arm around the teenager's shoulders and nodded. "Of course, Max. Go ahead."

"First, we'll begin with the smaller bequests. Each member of the estate staff will receive five thousand dollars for every year they've been employed. Adam's personal chauffeur will receive an additional twenty-five thousand dollars."

The family nodded in agreement, and Sandra smiled. Misty wasn't sure how they would have reacted if they hadn't agreed. There wasn't much they could do about it now.

"Adam's personal assistant Thomas Butler will receive the sum of fifty thousand dollars."

Tom looked like he wanted to stand up, hike a football in the end zone, but didn't want anyone to know how happy he was at the same time. His face was bright red and he was practically vibrating in his seat trying to hold his emotions in check.

"To his ex-wife Sandra Graham, I bequeath her main domicile, the house in San Francisco, and the sum of five hundred thousand dollars."

Sandra seemed quite content with that, murmuring something about Adam being a generous man but Misty couldn't make out all the words.

"To my companion Lydia Harrow, I bequeath the vintage Bentley that she currently drives and also the sum of twenty-five thousand dollars."

In contrast to the ex-wife, Lydia looked like she'd been slapped in the face. Multiple times. She wasn't happy at all.

Jared's hand tightened slightly on Misty's shoulder. He had to be noticing the rapid rise of tension in the room. The air was thick with it and she had to force herself to breathe normally and calm. Everyone was a hell of a lot jumpier than they'd been only five minutes ago. This wasn't as straightforward as Lydia had thought it would be.

"To my son David I bequeath my car collection, the house in Aspen, the house in Paris, and a third of my business portfolio including cash, stocks, bonds, and the Chipper Shopper corporation."

Despite his obvious hangover, David appeared quite happy with that outcome. If what Robin had said was true, he'd been expecting to be cut out of the family business.

"To my daughter Dahlia, I bequeath the house in Hawaii, the chateau in Switzerland, this house and all the furnishings, and a third of my business portfolio including cash, stocks, bonds, and the Chipper Shopper corporation."

Dahlia's expression barely changed at all. She could have received the best news in the world or the worst and no one would have known. She should have become a professional poker player.

"To my beloved granddaughter Taylor, I bequeath an apartment in New York City that I chose just for her. She will also receive the sum of five million dollars placed in a trust for her education. Once she turns twenty-five she can use it as she wishes."

Taylor was not pleased at all. She was frowning and hissing something to her grandmother that Misty couldn't make out. She kept shaking her head and Sandra kept trying to calm her down.

"That's bullshit," Taylor said loud enough for everyone to hear. "It's just stupid."

Sandra patted her granddaughter on the shoulder. "Hush, we'll talk about this later."

Taylor knocked Sandra's hand off her shoulder and silently fumed, crossing her arms over her chest.

"And to my newly-found daughter Misty Foster Monroe, I leave the house in Florida, the flat in London, and a third of my business portfolio including cash, stocks, bonds, and the Chipper Shopper corporation. I know that money cannot replace what you've missed out on not having a father, but I hope that this will in some way make up for not being there for you."

Chaos. Anarchy.

If Adam had jumped out from behind one of the heavy drapes and said *surprise!* it wouldn't have caused this much pandemonium. It was insane. Misty, however, hadn't said a word yet. She was numb. This couldn't be true. It had to be some sort of practical joke. It didn't make any sense at all.

There weren't words yet discovered to describe the screaming and the panic that had set in among the Reynolds family. No one was sitting quietly now except for Lydia and David. They seemed to enjoy watching the rest of them pace and yell.

Misty tugged at Jared's sleeve, pulling him down so she could whisper in his ear.

"We might want to make a run for it."

Because eventually they were going to stop yelling at Maximillian Sharp.

And turn their attention to the person they really hated.

Her.

CHAPTER NINETEEN

All hell had broken loose. There was yelling, stomping, some waving of arms, and shrill voices that made Jared want to cover his ears.

Of all the things he hadn't expected to happen today this would have been top of the list. What the fuck had Adam Reynolds been thinking? He clearly hadn't discussed this with anyone but his attorney and now his family was blindsided and pissed off. Reynolds really had been a son of a bitch right up until the end. He had to have known how they would react but he hadn't given a single damn.

Misty's fingers tightened on his arm. "We might want to make a run for it."

He'd already eyed the exit to the stairs and the dining room. Lydia and Tom were blocking it either by design or by accident. The French doors to the pool weren't a viable option either as Max Sharp was sitting almost right in front of them.

"You planned this," Taylor said, her face contorted with rage. "You convinced my grandfather to give my part of the company to you."

"That might be easier said than done, honey." He leaned

farther down so his lips were next to her ear. "Just tell them you won't take the money. Then they can all calm down."

She nodded, grabbing his hand and entwining their fingers.

"Please listen to me," Misty said loudly, rising from the chair. Jared followed her, keeping a hold of her hand. "Can you please quiet down for a minute? I want to say that I won't be accepting any money. I'm not going to take anything from Adam. This isn't what we came here for."

Everyone froze, their eyes round as if they hadn't heard her correctly. Clearly, no one had expected her to say those words. No one said anything until Dahlia stepped forward.

"You don't–I mean…you're not going to take the money?"

"I'm not going to take anything. I just wanted to meet my father. That's it. I never asked or wanted this."

"Well, that's fine then," Sandra said with a firm nod. "The company will be kept within the family."

Jared didn't bother reminding the older woman that Misty just might be family. They simply didn't know for sure yet.

Another clearing of the throat from Max. "Excuse me. I think I need to clear up a few things. Can you all sit down, please? There are things we still need to discuss."

They didn't want to, but Max Sharp simply gave them an expectant look and eventually everyone sat down, including Misty. Jared stayed standing, leaning on the wing of the chair.

"First of all, Adam wrote this will over two weeks ago. Before he had met Ms. Monroe. He told me all about their upcoming meeting and what he felt he owed her." Sharp rubbed at his pointed chin, his gaze running around the room before returning to the documents in front of him. "Second, he also anticipated his family's reaction and also Ms. Monroe's reluctance to accept her inheritance. He added this in his will. If Ms. Monroe refuses her bequest, all of his assets – every single one –

would be given to three charities he'd selected ahead of time. No one will get a single red cent. He was quite clear about that."

There was a second uproar among the family. Too many people talking loudly all at the same time.

Misty looked up at him, her eyes wide with panic. This was a shitshow of massive proportions and if Adam Reynolds were standing in from of Jared right now, he'd get a punch in the jaw for placing Misty in this position. It wasn't right or fair, but the asshole just had to have the last fucking word.

This was bullshit.

Taking his wife's hand, Jared gently pulled her away from the group so he could lead her back to their room. He was definitely taking her home in the morning. In fact, if he could convince her, he just might throw their things into suitcases and take her out of this house right the hell now. He could drive until it was dark and then check into a hotel for the night.

Misty seemed to instinctually understand what he wanted without him having to say a word, which was the best part of being married to someone for so long. He wasn't a man that liked to talk all that much and with her he didn't have to. Most times she knew exactly what he was thinking as if she could see the inner workings of his brain.

"I just wanted to get you out of there," Jared said as they exited the living room. "Adam should have warned you."

"I don't think he thought he was going to die so soon, but yes, I wish he'd given me a heads up. It was brutal in there. I actually felt the wave of hate coming off of them. I'd only heard about something like that in books, but it was real."

It certainly was. Jared had felt it too. If looks could kill and all of that.

When they were back in their room, Jared shut the door firmly behind them and flicked the lock closed. He didn't want anyone barging in on them to give Misty any more grief.

"Tell that attorney that you don't want their filthy money," he growled as Misty fell back on the bed, her head resting on a pile of pillows. "They're down there right now eating each other alive."

But then another thought occurred to him.

"Unless…sweetheart, do you want the money?"

Because if she did, he wouldn't stand in her way. In her mind, she might think that she deserved the inheritance since Adam had been a shitty, nonexistent parent and technically she wouldn't be wrong. She really did deserve the money. He'd sort of assumed that she wouldn't take it, though. It was too bad that the whole reading the mind thing didn't extend to him always knowing her thoughts too.

Plus Misty had been brought up on a shoestring, never having the resources for more than the bare essentials. When they'd married, he'd practically had to buy her an entire wardrobe and a new car. She was incredibly frugal as well, and she could squeeze a nickel like no one he'd ever known before. He often had to urge her to replace worn-out shoes and t-shirts with holes in them. She'd never cared much about material things. She'd simply laugh and tell him she'd just broken in those shoes so that they were comfortable.

Misty was already shaking her head, though. "No, I do not want the money."

"Because you do deserve it. He should have made sure that your mother had the support she needed to raise you."

"I still don't want it. We don't even know if he's my real father."

"Apparently, Adam was completely convinced. He did this before he even met you, and he clearly wanted you to have the money."

"Do we need it? We're fine, right?"

They were. Jared made an excellent living and honestly, so did she, although her income as an artist could swing wildly throughout the year. Plus he had his inheritance from his father passing away. Most of it was tied up in the ranch but they were doing fine.

"Absolutely, we don't have any money issues."

She sat up on the bed, wrapping her arms around her bent knees. "If I can't not accept the money, I guess we could put it in a trust for the kids."

"You don't have to accept it. You can make any choice that you want."

The idea of running a third of the business with Dahlia and David made Jared want to poke himself in the eye with a pen. Repeatedly. He couldn't imagine that it would be all that pleasant.

"If I don't accept then they won't get their inheritances."

"So? I'm not sure that would be the worst thing in the world," Jared argued. "They're horrible people, honey. Remember that one of them might have killed Adam. I'm not sure that they deserve millions of dollars."

"That's true," she conceded. "But they're not all guilty. I'd be robbing the rest of them, including the staff, and I'm not sure I can live with myself if I do that."

Jared was pretty sure that her generous, soft-hearted attitude was exactly what Adam had been banking on. He'd done his homework on his possible daughter and rolled the dice making out that will.

"It wouldn't be the end of the world if they had to get a job."

"You sound just like your father," Misty chuckled. "He was all about hard work shaping your character."

That was true. Gerald Monroe had taught his sons early that everything in this life had to be earned. Nothing was free. Nothing worth having, anyway.

"I'm not sure it would be the best thing for Lizzie and Nate to know that they had a few hundred million waiting for them when they grow up. I would imagine they might slack off a little bit. Or a lot."

"You make a good point. I swear my head hurts just thinking about it. My gut is telling me that this money would more of a curse than a gift. We don't need it, and you may be right about what it could do to the kids. We're so careful about spoiling them now. I can just hear Nate asking for a sports car when he graduates high school."

"He can ask all he wants, but he isn't getting one."

"So where does that leave us?"

"Charities, scholarship funds, hospitals. There's a hell of a lot of need out there. Even this much money won't solve it, but it could help."

She wrinkled her nose. "It will make the papers. People will find out."

After being the subject of cruel gossip in their hometown of Fielding, Misty wasn't a huge fan of others knowing her business. She liked to live quietly and privately. He did as well.

"It's going to make the news no matter what. A long-lost heiress to the Chipper Shopper fortune. Whether you give it away or not. You can always donate anonymously. But this will is definitely going to be news. If we're lucky, some politician will screw up and they'll take over the news cycle and everyone will forget about you."

"They might sue," Misty replied with a sigh. "Drag this through the courts for years."

"Then they'll be fighting the courts, not us. We don't even

need to get involved. I have a feeling though that Adam made sure his will was bulletproof. He was that kind of a man."

"I think coming here was a mistake. But I wanted to meet Adam. I wanted…"

Her voice trailed off but this time he already knew what she wanted to say. She'd wanted a father. Not for his money or anything like that. She wanted a human being that wasn't her children that was family. She was well aware that she couldn't change the past but she'd wanted Adam in her future.

She wasn't going to say it out loud, however.

Jared sat down on the bed next to her, nuzzling her temple. Her hair smelled like vanilla and coconut. "I'm so sorry, sweetheart. You deserved better."

She wrapped her arms around him, her lips pressed against his jaw. "I have better. You."

Somehow she always managed to take his breath away. He could see them in his mind's eye, old and gray but she could still turn him on with only the sound of her voice.

"We can leave here," he offered. "We don't have to wait until tomorrow morning. We can pack our bags and get out of here right now."

She looked tempted. Really tempted. But then she sighed, her shoulders slumping.

"We should be here when the town shows up to pay their respects. It would be wrong to go before that."

He held up a finger. "How about one hour and then we hit the road? We do the polite thing and then we make like a prom dress."

Misty's brows pinched together. "Like a prom dress?"

"You know…take off."

Rolling her eyes, she lightly slapped his shoulder. "Very funny. You're a real comedian."

"I was just trying to lighten the mood."

"It worked, and I'll take that deal. One hour. Then we leave."

He could deal with anything for an hour.

Even put up with the Reynolds family.

CHAPTER TWENTY

Misty was still reeling when she and Jared went downstairs later. People from the town were beginning to arrive and the staff had laid out a huge buffet of food and drink.

One hour. I can do this. Just one hour.

A video montage of Adam through the years was playing on the large screen television and Misty felt herself drawn to it, fascinated by the images of the man that might be her father.

"He was a handsome devil when he was younger, wasn't he?"

She turned to find Robin, the waitress from last night, standing behind her.

"He was," Misty agreed. "I didn't realize he was such an avid traveler."

There were photos of Adam at Machu Picchu, on a glacier in Alaska, and at the top of the Eiffel Tower among many other locations.

"I think he's been just about any place that a human can go," Robin replied. "Hell, I haven't been on the other side of the Mississippi. A big trip to me is down to Disneyland or Las Vegas."

Misty would have loved to have talked to him about all the places he'd been and the people he'd met. They'd never get a chance to do that now.

"So what are your plans? Are you going to be staying awhile?" Robin asked. "There's not much to do around here, to be honest."

"We're leaving today," Misty admitted. "We need to get home to our kids."

It wasn't bad as far as reasons went. Most people wouldn't question it.

"That's a shame, but I'm sure we'll be seeing you around. Next time you come to visit be sure to stop in the cafe. I can introduce you to more people in town."

Misty couldn't see why she would need to come back, but she didn't say so out loud. Instead, she thanked Robin and promised that the next time she was in town she would stop in.

It was the truth; she would stop in. But coming back was unlikely.

Robin drifted away and toward her friends. Eli had come in at some point and he and Jared were huddled together in the corner.

"You certainly have some nerve showing your face down here."

Lydia. Right up in Misty's face. The older woman's breath reeked of alcohol and her cheeks were red. She was holding a highball glass of brown liquid. Years of taking care of her own mother after a night of partying had given Misty a sensitive nose for booze. Lydia was drinking whiskey, and a lot of it by the looks of things.

I don't need this right now. I didn't ask for any of this.

"Lydia, maybe we should get you some black coffee."

And a cold shower to sober you up.

The older woman flung her arms in the air, liquid sloshing over the side of the glass and onto the floor. "I don't need any coffee. I'm fine. Just fine. I don't need the Reynolds family or any of you. I'm just fine on my own."

"That's good," Misty said in her most soothing tone. The one she used when her children were sick or crying. "I'm sure you can totally take care of yourself."

"I'll tell you this though." Lydia leaned in closer, her finger waving under Misty's nose. The air was filled with the stench of alcohol. "If Adam weren't already dead, I'd kill him myself. Do you hear me? I'd kill him with my bare hands."

The last was spoken loudly. Loudly enough for the guests to hear and the room grew quiet, everyone pausing their own activities to watch the meltdown.

Out of nowhere Tom was at Lydia's elbow, tugging her away in the general direction of the patio. "Come on, Lydia. How about some fresh air? I think that's just what we both need right now."

The other woman protested slightly but let Tom lead her away from Misty and slowly everyone went back to their drinks, food, and conversation.

"I hate being the center of attention," she whispered to Jared when he came to stand next to her. He was well aware of her aversion to attention so he must have made a beeline when he heard Lydia's voice. "Everyone was looking at me."

"To be fair, they were looking at Lydia, and for good reason. She seems to have imbibed a great deal of alcohol since the memorial service."

"She hates me. Everyone hates me."

"They don't hate you. They hate Adam."

"They're taking it out on me."

"Because he's not here. It won't do them any good, though.

Besides, you'll probably never see these people again. Does it matter what they think of you?"

Not really. She simply didn't like it when near strangers made up their minds without truly knowing her. It reminded her of when everyone in Fielding talked about her behind her back because of her mother's wild behavior.

"What the hell is going on there?" Jared asked, nodding toward an animated discussion between Sandra and Dahlia. Misty couldn't hear what they were saying from where they were standing, but Sandra was trying to step away and her daughter had a hold of her mother's arm and was pulling her back. Eventually, Sandra broke free and went to stand on the coffee table, clearing her throat to get everyone's attention.

"Attention, everyone. Attention, please. I have something to say and I want everyone to hear it."

Misty's fingers curled into Jared's arm, her heart slamming against her ribs. Was Sandra going to yell at Misty in front of all of these people? Was she going to accuse her of trying to convince Adam to give her an inheritance?

"Maybe we should get out of here," Misty said softly. "I don't like the look of this."

They didn't have a chance to slowly back out of the room, however. Sandra didn't pause at all, her voice breathless as if she'd just run a long distance.

"I need everyone to know something, and I cannot keep it to myself any longer. I killed Adam. I'm the one that hit him over the head. It was an accident. We were arguing. I didn't mean to do it, and that's why I've kept silent. I was afraid. But I'm the one that did it."

Misty could have heard a pin drop. It was as if the entire group of people were collectively holding their breaths. Then Eli made his way to the front of the room and held out his hand so that he could help Sandra down. When she was safely on the floor, he began to recite her Miranda rights.

It was over. Sandra had killed Adam.

Misty and Jared could go home.

Jared and Eli were sitting across from Sandra in the dingy, rundown interrogation room at the sheriff's station. The walls were gray, the table was gray, the floor tile was gray, hell, even the chairs were gray. If Eli wanted to depress the hell out of his suspects, then he was definitely on the right track.

Jared hadn't wanted to go with Eli, truth be told. He didn't think it was his place at this point. He'd agreed to help with the investigation, but that part was over. They were now getting an official confession. He didn't need to be here for that. He'd rather be on the road with Misty, heading home, but Eli had insisted that he see it through to the end.

"What did you argue about?" Eli asked. He was making a recording of the confession on a digital recorder.

Sandra shrugged. "The usual things. The kids, the house, the money. We fought all the time about various subjects. Adam thought he was always right and that he knew best about everything. He didn't care about anyone else's opinions. He ran roughshod over anyone standing in his way."

That sounded like the man that Jared had researched. Ruthless and arrogant.

"So lay it out for us," Eli said. "How did it happen?"

"We argued," Sandra repeated. "We were yelling and he was threatening to hit me. I reached for that stupid award in self-defense. You know...to scare him. Show him that I'd fight back this time. He turned his back and I hit him. I didn't mean to kill him. You have to believe that. I only meant to stop him from hurting me."

"Had he ever hit you before?" Jared queried.

"A few times. Adam had a temper."

"You never reported it?" Eli asked.

"I think these sorts of things should be kept between family, Sheriff."

There were more questions, trying to get down to the details of what had happened, and why she'd kept it a secret. Sandra had been concerned that no one would believe her claim of self-defense.

"I feared for my life, Sheriff."

Jared wasn't in any position to argue the point. He'd only met the family a few days ago.

Eli motioned to Jared and then quietly left the room, telling Sandra they'd be right back.

"Do you believe her?" Eli asked.

"I don't know. Do you *not* believe her? Why would she confess to a crime she didn't commit? I doubt a rich woman who has lived in comfort her entire life is looking forward to prison."

"I don't know. I just...I've known Sandra for years and while I believe she's capable of murder I hadn't pegged her for this one. She and Adam always appeared to get along fine."

"Looks can be deceiving, especially if he was physically and verbally abusive."

Eli shook his head. "Adam was going to be dead soon. It doesn't make any sense."

That was the part that had been bugging Jared the most. If anyone had wanted Adam dead, all they had to do was wait a short while.

"Then it doesn't make any sense for anyone to do it," Jared pointed out. "Anger can make people do funny things. If her story is true, I do feel for her."

"So do I. I'll have to keep her here until the county prosecutor decides what they want to do."

"Murder, manslaughter, or justified self-defense. Her story doesn't feel like a cold-blooded murder."

"I hope the prosecutor sees it that way. I've always liked Sandra."

"From what I've heard, Adam Reynolds could drive a saint to drink. Look at Lydia tonight. She was three sheets to the wind after the will reading."

"Now that's a woman that I could believe killed Adam," Eli declared. "She's stone cold, but she's not the one that confessed. Listen, I want to thank you for all your help. I know you didn't have to."

"I don't know that I was all that helpful. You didn't need me after all. You got your confession."

"I guess I did. I just wish I was happier about it. I guess you'll be heading out now?"

"Absolutely," Jared replied. "I asked Misty to pack while I was here. When I get back there, we're hitting the road. No offense, but I can't see this place in the rearview mirror fast enough."

"I don't blame you. You'll be missed, though. It was nice to have someone to work with for a change that really knew his stuff."

"Think about my offer and you can work with someone like that every single day."

Eli chuckled and shook Jared's hand. "I will think about it. You've made a compelling case. Safe travels, my friend. You never know. You just might hear from me one of these days."

Jared hoped that he did. Eli was a good man.

Now he could take Misty home. But there would be no forgetting this place or the Reynolds family in the near future.

His wife had gained and lost deeply this weekend. That was going to take some time to get over.

He'd be there for her. Forever.

CHAPTER TWENTY-ONE

I t was around noon the next day when Jared and Misty pulled into their own garage and unloaded the vehicle. Once they'd unpacked, Misty would start the laundry and Jared would run over to Reed and Kaylee's to pick up the kids.

They were both worn out, tired, and slightly confused about the last four days. They'd gone to see Adam Reynolds because she thought he might be her biological father, but it had turned into a disaster that she still hadn't quite processed.

Adam was dead.

His ex-wife had killed him.

He'd left Misty hundreds of millions of dollars that she'd have to somehow deal with.

She couldn't bring herself to deny the rest of the family their inheritance.

Shoving a load of clothes into the washer, she contemplated what to make for dinner. There wasn't much food in the house since they'd been out of town, but she always had chicken in the freezer so she could do something with that.

Jared joined her in the laundry room, the car keys jangling in his hand. "I'm going to get the kids and the pets now. Do you need anything while I'm out?"

She pressed the start button on the washer. "We need a full grocery shop, actually, but I doubt either of us is in the mood. I was just going to defrost some chicken. Not sure about what we'll have with it."

"We could just order a pizza."

The thought had occurred to her as well. "I would but I'm guessing that Lizzie and Nate have been partaking in a little bit of junk food over the weekend. I kind of felt like I should try and get a vegetable inside of them tonight."

Laughing, Jared nodded his head. "I bet they have been spoiled a bit, but I don't think one more pizza would send them on a path of juvenile delinquency."

"I'm not worried that they're going to knock over a liquor stand. I'm worried about their blood pressure and cholesterol."

Heaven knew no one had ever worried about Misty's health when she was a child. She'd eaten a massive amount of convenience food. She'd known how to use the microwave by her fifth birthday. By age seven, she could make the macaroni and cheese in a box.

"How about I cook the chicken on the grill?" Jared offered. "I know we have some frozen veggies in the freezer too. How's that for nutritious meal?"

"That sounds perfect."

Her husband walked toward the door to the garage but then paused. "Are you okay? You haven't said much since we left the estate yesterday."

They'd spent the night at a hotel along the way, getting up this morning and driving the rest of the trip. She hadn't said much because she didn't know what to say. It was all so surreal.

"I guess I'm still trying to process everything that happened. It's crazy, right? What we went through isn't normal."

"It isn't," he confirmed. "It is crazy, but it's over now. We're home and we can go back to our lives."

"We still have to deal with the money."

She didn't even want to think about the third of the business that she'd inherited. She planned to sell it to David and Dahlia if they wanted it. She assumed they would.

"We'll deal with it, but we don't have to make any decisions right away. We can take our time."

He was almost out the door when she spoke again.

"I'd like to go to Fielding, Jared. I want to visit my mother's grave."

If she'd surprised him, he didn't outwardly show it. But then this man was calm and steady personified. Even when all the madness was going on with Wade Bryson, he'd been like a port in a storm, always the voice of reason.

"We can do that. Whenever you like. School doesn't start for another six weeks."

They still had the house on the ranch from when they were first married.

"I've been thinking a lot about it," she explained. "Since getting that letter from Adam. I don't know why I need to be there. I just do."

"You don't need to give me a reason. We'll go this weekend if you like. The family will be thrilled to see the kids."

He was acting like it wasn't a big deal. But was it?

"Are you sure? We haven't been back since—"

"It's fine," he broke in, not letting her finish her sentence. She was going to remind him that they hadn't been back to Fielding since the funeral. "Ty's been busting my balls about visiting. It will be good to see everyone. You and Rayne can have some quality time together, and I'll get a chance to work on Dare about joining the consulting firm."

Work. Jared had certainly been doing a hell of a lot of that lately. He'd buried himself in it but then he had a passion for his career, just as she did. It was one of things that she loved so much about him, the way he dedicated himself to what he loved.

Like Misty and the children.

"If you're sure you can take more time away from the office, I'd like to go."

"I can work from Fielding if I need to. This is important."

"Good, then we'll go."

She had a few things to say to Annette Foster, and a few questions to ask. Of course, she wouldn't be getting any answers.

Misty would have to be content with that.

Jared parked the car under a shade tree in the quiet cemetery just outside of Fielding where both he and Misty had been brought up. It was a lovely sunny day and there was no one around, which only served to heighten his tension. He didn't like cemeteries much. His own mother and father were buried on the opposite side of the property along with a few Monroe cousins and an aunt.

"I'll wait here," he said to Misty. "Unless you want me to come with you."

Frowning, she cast a glance toward the far side of the property. "I thought you might…"

She didn't finish but then she didn't have to. He knew exactly what she was referring to. She thought he might take the opportunity to go visit his parents' graves.

"Not today. You can take your time, honey. I'll go through my email and messages."

She gave him a strange look but he ignored it, pulling out his phone and beginning to scroll through the myriad of emails that he received each day. Misty exited the vehicle and he looked up to watch her walk the short distance to her mother's grave. She'd brought flowers and she'd placed them near the small headstone before sitting on the green grass cross-legged.

He had things he should be doing but he couldn't drag his gaze away from his wife sitting at her mother's grave. At one point she reached into her pocket and pulled out her phone, scrolling and then holding it up as if showing Annette Foster something on the screen.

Photos of their children? The dog? The cat? The house? Perhaps. He didn't know the last time Misty had been here. Had she visited regularly before they moved? He was bothered by the fact that he didn't know this one fact about his wife. Did it make her feel better to talk to her mother? Their relationship had been complex to say the least. Misty had loved Annette, but the woman hadn't been the greatest mother. It spoke to how deeply his wife could forgive that she didn't hold a grudge regarding her upbringing. She always spoke of it matter-of-factly. But then again, when they'd first met she'd always expected the worst from people. Now she had a much more optimistic view of human nature.

Before he knew it, Misty was walking back to the car. He checked the digital clock on the dash and was surprised to see that forty minutes had gone by. It hadn't felt that long. She climbed into the vehicle, tucking her phone into her purse which she'd left on the passenger side.

"Okay, we can go."

That was it? She wasn't going to say anything about it?

"Do you want to talk? I'm here if you want to."

She shook her head. "Not right now. Later."

Since meeting her father, she'd kept telling him she was processing.

They drove back to the ranch and Jared pulled up to the main house where Ty was living with his husband Kyle. He hadn't wanted to take over, happy with his smaller home close to Jared's but Royce had been adamant that he didn't want to live there. They hadn't wanted to let the house go empty and unused either, so eventually Ty and Kyle had decided to move in about three months after their father had passed away.

What Jared hadn't expected – but should have – was that Ty and Kyle would make changes to the house and its decor. When they'd arrived last night with the kids for dinner, he'd been shocked to see a brand-new kitchen and updated bathrooms. The carpets had been taken up and gleaming hardwood had been put in their place. His mom's knickknacks had been taken down and replaced with photos and more modern framed paintings. Kyle had an artist friend in New York City, and he'd done several of the paintings throughout the house as a wedding gift.

Even their old couch had been replaced with a new leather set. Silently, Jared mourned the loss of his childhood memories. In every nook and cranny of this house, every stain on the carpet and sofa, he had a memory that made him smile. What an amazing childhood he'd had.

Kyle had Lizzie, Nate, and their dog outside. Misty dropped a kiss on Jared's cheek before rushing out to join them. Ty grabbed two beers from the refrigerator and held one out to Jared.

"You look like you could use one of these."

"I could. What's your excuse?"

"I won't let you drink alone. I'm a humanitarian that way."

"Like Ghandi."

"Fuck, yeah."

Accepting the bottle, Jared twisted off the cap and took a

long draw. The cold liquid felt good on his parched throat.

"How was it?" Ty asked, leaning a hip against the brand-new marble countertop. There was a copper backsplash and fresh white cabinets.

"It was fine. She talked to her mother for a little while and then we came home."

Something flickered across Ty's expression, but it was gone in an instant. "What did she say?"

"I don't know. She talked with Annette alone."

"You didn't go with her?"

"No, it was personal, obviously."

Ty took another drink from his beer. "Maybe she might want the support."

"Maybe she wanted to do this herself," Jared countered. "This isn't the kind of thing that you share with a spouse. We weren't going for ice cream or buying a new sofa."

Ty's brows shot up. "So we finally get down to it. I was wondering when you were going to bring it up. I saw your expression last night when you walked in. Go ahead, big brother. Tell me that I've changed your shrine of a childhood home."

Jared didn't like his little brother's mocking tone. He also didn't like that he was so fucking transparent that Ty knew that he didn't like the changes.

"I don't care," Jared replied as blandly as possible. "You can do whatever you want to the house."

"Thank you for acknowledging that."

But...

"I just think you might have given us a heads up or something. We might have had input."

"Input? What do you mean?"

Ty's tone was dangerous, as if he might go off any second, but Jared wasn't going to take any shit from him since he was the one that brought up the new decor to begin with.

"This is our family home. That's all I'm saying."

Ty slapped his bottle onto the counter. "So you have a home here on the ranch and one outside of Seattle, and I don't get a say in what you do to those, but somehow you get a say in what I do here. We agreed that this was going to be mine and Kyle's home. I didn't realize that it came with strings."

"It doesn't come with—"

"Then why are you talking about getting your fucking input? Why do you think you get a say in how I decorate my goddamn house?"

The heat had built up on the back of Jared's neck and the next words out of his mouth were not what he had intended to say.

"Because it's our goddamn house. Everything is goddamn changed."

Groaning, Ty scraped his fingers through his hair. "Everything changes. Eventually."

"I don't like it," Jared shot back. He needed to keep his mouth shut but for the life of him he couldn't seem to do it. Words were falling out of his mouth at a rate he couldn't stem. "Everybody says that change is inevitable, but I think that's bullshit. It's bullshit, Ty."

There was a long stretch of silence where neither of them said anything. Jared tried to breathe deeply and calm himself down, but it wasn't working. For whatever reason, he was angry and at this point he didn't care. He had no fucks left to give.

Eventually Ty spoke first.

"I know that you're not taking any of this very well—"

"*Any of this.* What does that mean?"

"You know what it means."

"Apparently, I don't. Do please enlighten me."

He sounded like a sarcastic shit because he was one.

"Fine," Ty replied, his own tone aggressive. "You're not dealing with Dad's death very well. You're not dealing with any of the changes that his death brought on. You're not dealing with shit which is just your way. You think you can ignore the shit out of something, and it will all just eventually go away. Well, reality sucks, man. It doesn't work like that. Dad will still be dead next month, next year, and next decade. You can pretend he's not all you want but you're only fooling yourself. The rest of us have to live in the real world. You can go into your man cave and play cops and robbers and leave us little people to deal with it all."

Ty had never been closer to getting his face punched out than this moment. Jared's fist itched to connect with his pretty-boy brother's jaw, but his wife and kids were twenty feet away on the other side of a flimsy screen door.

"I deal with things."

Ty snorted, a grin spreading across his face. "No, you don't. Do you even hear yourself talk? You went to the cemetery where our parents are buried, and you didn't even visit their graves. You didn't take flowers. You didn't do shit. Did you ever think about going over and talking to them? It might make you feel better."

Jared couldn't imagine how any of that would make him feel even the tiniest bit better. This was a bunch of crap and he didn't have to take his brother's bullshit about it.

"Dad and Mom aren't even there," he heard himself saying. "It's only their bodies and a headstone. I'm not talking to a fucking stone."

His throat had choked up at the end, the words strangled as they came out. He was close to stomping out of the room, but he didn't know where to go. There was no escape in this house;

his past was here even with new floors and paint.

"So talk to Dad and Mom wherever you are," Ty suggested. "I have some of my best conversations with them while I'm sitting on the back porch in the evening after dinner and drinking a beer. You're right, bro. Mom and Dad aren't in a cemetery, they're everywhere that we are. We're their legacy. Us. Don't you feel them watching over us? I do. I feel it every day. Maybe because I'm here on the ranch. They might hate Seattle for all I know."

Ty was trying to make a joke, but it fell flat. Jared wasn't in the mood to laugh or even smirk. He was far down the rabbit hole and only getting deeper.

"You talk to them?"

"Sometimes. When I have questions or have something to say."

"Do they answer?"

His question came out almost a whisper, but his brother heard him loud and clear.

Chuckling, Ty nodded. "Not in the way you think. I don't hear voices or anything, but I feel better. I guess that's an answer. To me, anyway."

"Kyle doesn't think you're crazy?"

"Kyle is crazy so we're a perfect match. Is that what this is? You think that Jared Monroe is too dignified and mature to talk to himself?" Ty rubbed at the back of his neck. "Do you think it was easy? Doing this? Tearing up the carpet that we spilled Kool Aid on and getting rid of the couch where we made forts? Let me tell you, asshole, it wasn't. I cried like a fucking baby for days. Kyle was a saint for all of it too. He kept saying that we didn't need to change anything, even though he and I both knew that all this stuff desperately needed to be replaced. At first, it was like I was throwing out all of our childhood but then I realized that I still remembered it. All of it. I didn't need a stained couch to keep that in my heart. Neither do you, Jared. It was just stuff. Things. I didn't get rid of what really mattered. Family. It's what matters. It's *all* that matters."

"I know that."

He sounded defensive though, which was the last thing he wanted to be.

"I know you know. I just think that you're hurting, and you've forgotten it a little."

Jared was already shaking his head before his brother had finished speaking.

"I'm not hurting. You don't need to worry about me. I just have a lot on my plate. I'm worried about Misty. She's been through so much."

Straightening, Ty walked over to the screen door, his gaze on Kyle, Misty, the kids, and the barking dog running around the yard and laughing.

"I do worry about Misty, but I worry about you too."

"You don't have to."

"I'm your brother. I get to whether you like it or not."

Fair enough, but Ty was wasting his time. Jared was fine. Busy as hell, with plenty of responsibilities, but fine.

He could take care of everything and everyone, and still take care of himself. That's what a man did, right?

He had it all under control.

CHAPTER TWENTY-TWO

J ared had been acting strangely since their visit to the cemetery. Misty had half-expected it, to be honest. She'd been feeling that he hadn't really dealt with his father's death this past year, stuffing his feelings way down and hoping they'd simply go away. It wasn't, however, a subject that she could lecture him on because she wasn't so sure that she'd dealt with her own parent's death. Now with Adam's passing, it had all come up again.

She was beginning to wonder whether a loved one's death was something that she was even supposed to "get over" at all. Perhaps there would always be a little bit of pain whenever she was reminded. It might not be a bad thing. She didn't want to forget Annette Foster or Adam Reynolds. They were both important to her, although for far different reasons.

The kids were in bed and Jared was puttering around in the kitchen, pouring them each a glass of wine. They'd eaten dinner with his family at the main house and she always enjoyed seeing Ty, Kyle, and Royce.

But it was nice to have some quiet time, just the two of them. In their busy lives, they didn't get much chance to simply relax and spend time together. Even now, Jared had worked on his laptop for a few hours before dinner.

He padded out of the kitchen on bare feet and handed her a glass of Chardonnay. They were both dressed casually in sweatpants and t-shirts, although Misty's feet were covered with comfy socks to keep her toes warm. Jared had offered to light a fire in the fireplace as it cooled down so much at night, but she'd told him not to bother.

He sat down on the couch and she leaned into him so he could curl around her, her head cushioned on his chest. The wine would make her drowsy and with any luck she'd fall asleep right here in her husband's arms.

They were quiet for a long time, but she could practically hear the wheels in Jared's head turning.

"Something on your mind, handsome?"

He didn't say anything for a long time, but his embrace tightened and he dropped a kiss on her temple. His breath was warm on her cheek and she reached up to caress his stubbled jaw.

"What did you say to your mother today?" he finally asked, his voice soft as if he didn't want anyone to overhear. "You don't have to tell me if you don't want to. I know it's personal."

It was personal but she was fine with talking to him about it. There were few people on this planet that she could say that about. Him and Rayne. That was about it.

"I can talk about it. I told my mother what has been going on in my life. About you and the kids, and the dog, and the cat, and my painting, and then I finally told her about Adam. I asked her if she thought he was my biological father. I asked her if she loved him, and if she ever thought to tell him she was pregnant. I told her that he died, but that he was nice to me."

He didn't say anything else, seemingly digesting her words.

"I didn't expect her to answer me or anything," she said.

"But it made me feel better to talk to her even though it was one-sided. I hadn't visited Mom's grave for a long time."

"I wondered about that."

"It was after we were married. I brought Lizzie to show her. I know it's sort of silly, but it does make me feel like she's sort of there even though she'd been gone for so long."

"Ty says he talks to Dad and Mom. Not at the cemetery, but on the back porch. He says he feels like Mom and Dad are all around, watching over him."

Her poor husband. He didn't have a clue how to deal with his emotions most of the time. Gerald had drilled into his children that they shouldn't show them. As the youngest Ty had received less of that message and his personality simply wasn't the type to hide what he was feeling all of the time. Jared, on the other hand, was the middle child and as such he worked to not make waves. Emotions upset people and that was something he didn't like to do.

"And you don't feel that way?" she guessed, running her fingertips on the bare skin of his arm in what she hoped was a soothing motion. He was all tied up in knots lately.

Since the letter had shown up and reminded him about Gerald. Up until then, he'd successfully ignored his own grief and pain.

"I guess that I don't."

"Do you *want* to feel that way?"

"I don't know. Sometimes. I just don't know how I would talk to them when they're not here."

"If you're alone there's no one to judge you," Misty pointed out. "No one is going to tell you that you're doing it wrong. I don't think there is a right or wrong way, honestly. Just talk to them."

"About what?"

"I don't know. The price of groceries. The weather. How bad traffic is or the funny things the kids say all the time. Anything that you would have talked to them about before."

"We talked about the ranch. Or my job, mostly."

"Then talk to them about that. They're not in a position to complain. This is about you."

She'd tried to lighten the mood, so she was glad to hear Jared chuckle a bit.

"I guess they're not. That would be a switch. Dad always had something to say whenever we talked."

"Then think of this as a chance to say all the stuff that you always wanted to."

He leaned down and brushed his lips over hers, sending a jolt of pleasure up her spine.

"You're a great wife, do you know that?"

"Yes."

She felt the rumble of laughter in his chest next to her ear. "I bet you do."

"You're a pretty decent husband too."

"I try. You know there isn't anything that I wouldn't do for you and the kids."

She did know that. He showed her how important they were every single day.

"Then can I ask you a question?"

She'd been thinking about this and it wouldn't go away.

"You can, of course. What do you need?"

"I'm not sure I need anything except to talk to you about Adam's death." He stiffened and she sat up, turning so that they were face to face. "It's not anything bad. At least I don't think so. It's just...damn."

"Go ahead," he urged. "It's just what?"

"It's just that I'm having a hard time dealing with Sandra's confession. I just…I don't get why she'd do it. Not after all these years. He was going to die in a few months. It doesn't make any sense."

"It doesn't make any sense for anyone to kill him."

"It makes even less sense for her to do it. She'd been putting up with him for so long. She didn't tell us anything specific that made her snap that night. There was nothing out of the ordinary."

"They argued. And he was abusive."

"When they were married. That was a long time ago."

"He was a total bastard," Jared reminded her. "He kept her from her own children supposedly."

"I just don't get the murderer feeling from her," Misty said with a sigh.

"Did you get that feeling with anyone else?"

"David," she admitted. "I got it from him. Also Tom. He had a whole bunch to hide."

"Do you know how much I love you? Do you have any idea?"

"I think I do. I love you that much too."

She wasn't sure why he was changing the subject, but she always enjoyed telling him how much she loved him. She liked hearing it back too.

"I love you so much that I'll call Eli and ask him to send me the files for Adam's murder."

For a moment she was confused as to why he would do that, but then it hit her. He was going to see if there was enough evidence to support or not support Sandra as the killer.

"You'd really do that?" She wasn't sure how to explain her feelings about this. "I know it's a long shot but… If Sandra didn't really do it, then it's not really justice, is it? It's empty and meaningless. Adam may have been a bad person, but I don't think anyone deserves to be murdered. He was trying to make amends. He was trying to be better."

"I'll call Eli in the morning. You're right. If Sandra isn't really the one that did it, then it isn't true justice."

"But you think she did it."

"I don't know if she did or not. She confessed. Innocent people usually don't confess to murder, but it has been known to happen although under different circumstances. She wasn't being interrogated and pressed. She stepped up during a party and she wasn't accused of anything. What was her motivation to do that? I guess that might be a good place to start looking."

"You don't have to do this if you don't want to. I'm probably making this a bigger deal than it really is." Jared already had a desk full of work. He didn't need her tasking him with more. "Now I feel guilty."

"You want to make it even? How about you make your famous lemon Bundt cake? Looking through a case file for some of that cake is totally worth it."

"I'll make you the best lemon cake ever. Heck, I'll make one every week for a month."

"Deal. And I'm getting the better end."

Maybe, maybe not. A second look.

If Sandra was guilty, why did she confess? And if she was innocent...it made even less sense.

Did Sandra kill Adam? And why?

If anyone could find the answers, it was Jared Monroe.

CHAPTER TWENTY-THREE

Two days later Jared was sitting at his desk staring at his
computer screen. Eli had easily agreed to send up the entire
case file. It turned out that the lawman was of the same mind as
Misty. Sandra as the killer didn't make sense. In these last few
days, as Jared had turned the case over and over in his mind, he
was in agreement.

It didn't make any damn sense for Sandra to step on that
coffee table in the middle of the wake and announce that she
was the murderer. She wasn't even under that much suspicion.
Sure, she had motive but so did a hell of a lot of people. As
Misty had said, after all these years why didn't she just wait for
Adam's cancer to run its course?

His partner Jason stuck his head into the office. "You're here
early. I thought I'd beat everybody in today."

"You and I could never beat Logan. I swear that man never
sleeps. He already had a pot of coffee brewing when I arrived."

Jason strolled into Jared's office, steaming coffee cup in
hand.

"You're frowning."

"I probably am," Jared agreed. "I'm taking a second look at

the evidence in the Adam Reynolds case."

Jason's brows shot up in surprise. "I thought you had a confession."

"Misty, Eli, and I aren't exactly convinced that Sandra did it."

Settling himself into a guest chair, Jason peered at the computer screen. "Then why would she confess to a crime she didn't commit? Do you think she's covering for someone?"

"That's what I'm thinking. She has two children and one of them had an especially strong motive – her son David. He made no secret of his contempt for his father and the family in general."

Jason took another sip of his coffee. "So what do you need me to do? How can I help?"

It was Jared's turn to be surprised. "I didn't expect you to have time to help me."

"I'll make time." Jason pointed to the screen. "Can you print some of this up for me? You know I'm old school."

"I can. Maybe you could do a deeper dig on the background searches for the family members? We don't have much here, to be honest. Forensics found a button and we have some video from the front gate of the estate. I'm hoping to enhance that to see if perhaps we missed someone on foot in the dark. There was a palmprint on the French doors, but Eli ran it. No match."

"Did everyone in the house submit their prints for comparison?"

"That would be a no," Jared laughed. "He suggested it and they balked. On the advice of an attorney. He hopes that eventually he'd have a suspect to compare."

"And does Sandra Reynolds match?"

"No, and that's one of the reasons Eli has doubts."

Leaning forward, Jason stroked his chin. "The prints not

matching may not mean anything at all. It could that the print was made by someone else at a different time. It does raise questions, though."

"Supposedly, the glass was cleaned inside by one of the housekeepers that morning. The print was on the inside."

"Sometimes people say they did something, but they really didn't. They might have been pressed for time and didn't want to admit that they cut a few corners. Or maybe they did clean the glass and another member of the family or staff put the print there and it's completely unrelated. That's why they clean the glass in the first place. It gets dirty."

"So you can see where we are here," Jared replied. "Sandra confessed, but her motive was murky and certainly not the strongest."

"You and I both know that people have been murdered for a pack of smokes. Motive is personal. If they think it's enough of a reason, then it is. You're leaning to the son, though?"

"David Reynolds. Let's just say he has issues with his father. His rifle might also have been used to scare the horses that his sister and niece were riding."

"Might have?"

"We don't have anything to match it to," Jared explained. "His rifle had been recently fired but he said that he'd done some shooting practice."

"That's not a very efficient way to kill someone."

"Agreed, it feels more like a scare tactic. Just like Misty and I getting locked in the garage. There were about a dozen tools in there that we could use to get out."

"Where was he when you were trapped in the garage?"

"He said he was upstairs in his room getting dressed for the memorial service. No one saw him downstairs, either. But he could have started those cars remotely."

"He couldn't have locked you in and cut the power remotely, though," Jason observed. "Do you think he has a partner?"

"Town gossip says he's seeing a local woman, but as far as we know she hasn't set foot on the estate. We checked the gate footage and no one except the staff came in that morning."

"Are there other ways to get on the property?"

"Only by horseback. Doesn't mean that they didn't come in that way, it's just tougher."

"I think the first thing they should do is update the damn security on the estate," Jason said. "It's far too lax for a family that has so many assets."

"I agree but Adam apparently didn't like a lot of modern technology. He felt that if anyone really wanted to get to him, they would."

"He has a point, but still…"

Jared held up his hands in surrender. "Trust me when I say that I don't think the family would listen to me about anything, so telling them to get more security is a waste of time. They don't want me or Misty around there ever again. When we drove away that afternoon, I could almost hear the cheer that went up as we exited the property."

Jason laughed. "They were that charming, huh?"

"Let's just say that I don't have any doubts that one of them did this."

And Jared was determined to find out the truth.

Because Misty was right. If Sandra really wasn't the killer, then true justice hadn't been served.

It was later that day when Jason came back to Jared's office. He was wearing a triumphant grin and holding up a piece of paper.

"You better have the evidence to back up that expression,"

Jared warned him. "And I have news too."

Chuckling, Jason sat down after placing the paper on Jared's desk. "Tom has officially resigned Chipper Shopper and is going to another competitor. He's rented a house on the outskirts of Dallas and is already out of the one in California. He and his family moved out under the cover of darkness. According to the neighbors, the family was there one day and gone the next. I think that's behavior worthy of a second look. I also found a female that used to work at Chipper Shopper who apparently had a relationship with him last year. She left the company and broke it off. I think she might be someone you want to talk to."

"How did you–" Jared broke off and simply shook his head in amazement. Jason didn't dig into the research details often but when he did, he was a hell of an investigator. "Never mind, I'm just going to put it down to all the contacts you have all over the states. I think you have friends in every square inch of this country and a few others too."

"It's good to have friends."

"I can't argue with that sentiment. It's funny that you brought me some information about Tom because I finally ran down the details on that button forensics found. It's a standard white shirt button used mainly on off the rack, discount clothing. Not something that a Reynolds family member would wear."

Jason's smile widened. "But one of their employees might. Your friend Tom has been doing an awful lot of lying. I think he's someone of interest in this case."

Except for one thing...

"I'd agree but I can't imagine why Sandra would confess to a murder that Tom committed," Jared mused out loud. "I could understand one of her own children, but Tom?"

"Maybe Tom got to her too?" Jason suggested. "You said he was romancing mother and daughter. He might have been romancing the grandmother as well."

Jared rubbed the back of his neck. "Holy shit, that's a possibility. What was he thinking?"

"He was thinking that he might just hit the jackpot with one of them. He was playing the odds and the more women, the better chance that one might actually fall for him."

"That makes me want to puke. I feel for his wife and kids. They're innocent in all of this."

"And Tom isn't innocent at all. Have you had a chance to work on the video yet?"

"A little bit but there's still more to do. I was hoping to see someone on foot, maybe in the shadows but so far nothing."

Jason stood and slapped Jared on the back. "You'll find it. Now I'm going to go back and see what else I can dig up. I'll check in with you later."

After grabbing a soda from the office refrigerator, Jared sat back down at his desk and began working on the video again, using a few borrowed algorithms to enhance the darker areas of the recording. The camera that Adam Reynolds was using at his gate wasn't the latest and greatest model, but it was decent enough to make out most of the details on the main driveway. Problem was the edges were murky and slightly blurred.

He was painstakingly going through the video, frame by frame, and his shoulders were getting tight while a headache bloomed behind his eyes. Taking a break, he stretched and yawned, picking up his now empty can of soda and drinking the very last drops at the bottom.

Taylor's new car zooming out through the front gate was the next frame up and he worked around the edges but found nothing. Again.

As he had with each frame before, he also enhanced the center of the image even though it was quite clear. He was able to zero in on the car and the passengers and out of habit he counted the people in the vehicle – and the three cars that followed on Taylor's heels leaving the property – and compared it to the number that had been at the party.

Wait…it didn't match. It didn't *fucking* match.

He reversed the recording and counted the people in the vehicles once again.

Two were missing. But who? He'd have to enhance the recording even more to be able to see their faces. Could one of these teenagers have killed Adam? And why?

He had to really zero in on the interior of the cars to be able to make out the faces, and that took quite a bit of time. The sun was down outside when he looked up from his laptop and realized that it was Brent who wasn't in any of the vehicles.

But even more…

The driver of Taylor's brand-new birthday car didn't look like Taylor when he'd zoomed in close on the face and cleared up the distortion. It was the other young female, Cara. She was wearing Taylor's jacket. Jared assumed that Taylor had traded it for the young woman's cardigan.

Taylor had specifically made it look like she was driving out of the front gate for the cameras, but she and Brent hadn't left the estate that night.

It was beginning to make some sense. If Sandra had any inkling that her granddaughter might have killed Adam, that would be a powerful motive to confess to the crime.

Jared's hand was reaching for the phone when Jason stuck his head around the door.

"I might have found something of interest."

"Is it about Brent Carson?"

"Are you psychic now? Yes, it is. How did you know?"

"I can show you," Jared said, pointing to his screen. "Looks like a couple of teenagers were playing a little hide and seek with us."

Cueing up the recording, Jared pointed out the number of people and then his enhancement of the driver of Taylor's new car.

"Taylor and her boyfriend hung back for some reason and didn't want anyone to know about it. They specifically told Eli that they'd left the estate with their friends and that she didn't get back until after the body was found. The only thing I'm stuck on here is motive. From what everyone said, Taylor adored her grandfather and he felt the same about her. He was very indulgent with her and gave her anything she wanted."

Jared held up the paper in his hand. "I think I might be able to help with that. I dug into Tom's background but really didn't found anything more. So I worked through your list and ended up with Brent Carson. It turns out his cousin worked for Chipper Shopper and was fired by the store manager about three months ago. Maybe this was revenge."

"That gives Brent motive but what about Taylor? Why would she take part?"

Jason shrugged. "Perhaps she held back to try and stop him. Or she might have taken part because she loved him. A first love burns hot and fast. I know I did stupid shit when I was in love for the first time."

"You didn't kill any of your family," Jared pointed out. "That's a bridge too far."

"Then perhaps she did stay behind to try and stop him."

"Then why didn't she just tell somebody?" Jared asked, more to himself than to his friend. "If she didn't want Brent to get in trouble, she could have just told her mother or Sandra."

"What are you going to do?"

"Call Eli," Jared replied immediately. "We need to talk to

Cara, the girl that Taylor switched jackets with. Then we need to talk to Taylor and Brent. Probably Sandra as well."

They finally had a clue they could follow.

CHAPTER TWENTY-FOUR

"I don't think that I have to talk to you," Cara said, her fingers nervously twisting the hem of her shirt. "There are laws about this, right?"

They were all sitting in her living room – Jared, Eli, Cara, and her mother. Unlike the Reynolds estate, this home was a more middle-class ranch style with a two-car garage and a minivan in the driveway. It reminded Jared of the one that Misty drove at home.

"You have the right to an attorney," Eli agreed. "I've already read you your rights. You can remain silent if you wish, Cara."

Cara's mother placed her hand on her daughter's shoulder. "Cara doesn't have anything to hide. Do you, honey?"

The mother might be sure of that, but the daughter appeared visibly shaken by Jared and the sheriff's visit.

"Mom," Cara pleaded, not meeting Jared's gaze. Her foot was bouncing up and down and she looked ready to jump out of her skin. She was scared. "I made a promise."

She whispered the last four words but both Jared and Eli heard it.

"Did you promise Taylor and Brent?" Eli prompted. "Did

they ask you to drive her new car out of the gate, wearing Taylor's jacket?"

Cara's body language seemed to collapse upon itself, her arms wrapping themselves around her torso, her shoulders slumping, and her head hanging down. She didn't need to verbally answer the question. Her body had done it for her.

"We need the whole story, Cara," Eli said, leaning forward trying to establish eye contact. "Because if you didn't trade jackets, then the button we found underneath Adam Reynolds' dead body might belong to your cardigan. That would make you a suspect in his murder. The main suspect."

Her head shot up, her eyes wet with tears. "I didn't kill anybody. You have to believe me."

"We do believe you," Jared said. "But you have to tell us the truth."

It was dawning on the mother what was going on and her expression was horrified, her face pale.

"Cara Louise, you tell them the truth right now." Her mother's voice sounded anguished and a few tears rolled down her cheeks. "My God, what have you done?"

"It was just a favor for Taylor," Cara replied, her voice still small. "She said it was just a joke. I didn't know they were going to do anything bad. She said it was just a prank, that's all. I never thought—"

Cara broke off, the words choked off when the sobs took over. Her mother gathered her daughter close, rocking her to calm the teenager.

"You need to tell them everything," she insisted. "Every detail and don't leave anything out. I never trusted that Taylor Reynolds. She was too wild and didn't listen to anyone."

"Start at the beginning," Eli suggested. "When did she first bring up switching clothes?"

Once they knew all the details, they'd need to talk to Taylor and Brent.

Had she really murdered her own grandfather? And why?

✧ ✧ ✧ ✧

Misty sat on the back patio by the pool at the Reynolds estate. She hadn't planned on ever returning there, but the universe had other plans. She sipped her iced tea and nibbled on the slice of lemon cake that one of the kitchen staff had given her. Her stomach was tumbling in her abdomen, but she was determined to keep her outer facade cool and calm.

"Linda, can you–"

Dahlia had just walked outside but stopped abruptly when she saw Misty sitting there.

"Oh, I didn't see you. I thought I heard Linda out here."

"She was here," Misty replied. "She brought me a piece of cake and some iced tea, but I think she's back in the kitchen now."

"Fine." Dahlia took a step but then hesitated. "I wasn't aware that you were returning to the house."

"It was a last-minute decision. My husband Jared drove down here to talk to Sheriff Eli."

"Oh." Dahlia looked confused. "What about?"

"Adam's death."

Now the other woman was more confused than ever.

"What about Dad's death? The case is closed."

"He's not so sure that your mother murdered your father."

Staggering back, Dahlia grabbed onto a chair for support. "Are you kidding? Don't tell me that this is some sort of joke."

"It's not a joke. He's quite serious about this. He doesn't think that Sandra did it."

Dahlia pressed her hands to her cheeks, looking ready to cry.

"I kept saying that I didn't think my mother could do something like this. I kept saying that there was something more."

Misty nodded in agreement. "Jared thinks that she was covering for someone."

"Covering for someone," Dahlia echoed, her brow furrowed. "Who on earth would she be covering for?"

"That's a good question."

Misty was watching the other woman's reactions closely. What did she know? Was she covering up as well?

Dahlia sagged and grabbed the back of a chair again. "Oh dear, not...David?"

"You think your brother did this?"

"I don't want to," Dahlia replied, her voice faint. "I know he can get angry, though. He and Dad fought a lot."

Misty didn't get a chance to reply. Eli had stepped out onto the patio wearing an all-business expression.

"Ladies, can you please join us in the living room? We're about to get started."

"The living room? What's getting started?" Dahlia asked.

Misty had already been briefed. She placed her cake and iced tea down on the small side table and stood.

"Eli has questions for all of us."

Eli and Jared had gathered the entire family – Lydia, David, Taylor – and now Misty and Dahlia. Misty went to sit in an armchair close to where Jared was standing, and Dahlia sat next to Taylor. David was standing near the liquor bar and Lydia was sitting near the empty fireplace.

Eli glanced at Jared before beginning.

"We have a few more questions about the night Adam was murdered," Eli announced. "We're hoping that you can help us."

"What sort of questions, Sheriff?" Lydia asked. "I thought this case was solved."

"They think that Mother didn't do it," Dahlia piped up. "They think she's covering for someone else."

"Someone else?" David repeated. "Like who?"

"Like you," Dahlia shot back. "You had more motive to kill Dad than anyone here. You hated him."

"I may have hated him, but I didn't kill him," David said defensively. His hand automatically reached for the whiskey bottle and an empty highball glass. "I would never kill my own father."

"So you think our mother did?"

Clearing his throat, Eli continued. "Can we ask the questions, please?"

Jared pulled out some notes from his shirt pocket. "Now let's go through that evening again. The party broke up and...Lydia?"

"I went upstairs," she said. "I watched some television and then fell asleep. When I woke up, Adam wasn't there so I went downstairs to check on him. That's when I found him."

"And David? What did you do?"

"I had some more to drink and blacked out on the back patio on a lounge chair. I didn't see my father after he went into his office with Tom."

"Right. And Dahlia, you also went upstairs to bed, correct?"

The woman nodded. "I went to speak with the kitchen staff. That lasted about thirty minutes and then I went upstairs. I read a book and then went to bed about eleven-thirty."

Jared checked something off on his list. "Now Misty and I also went upstairs, watched some television, and then fell asleep."

This is it.

Misty shook her head. "That's not all. Remember what you saw when you looked out our bedroom window? Right when we were settling down to watch television."

Tapping the paper with his paper, Jared nodded his head. "Right, right. When I looked out the window, I saw Tom and Dahlia kissing on the back patio."

Taylor leaped to her feet, her eyes wide and her face red. "What? You were kissing Tom? Oh my God, Mother. Why did you kiss him? How long have you been kissing him?"

"Calm down, Taylor," Lydia jumped in before Dahlia could reply. "They were two adults kissing. It's no big deal. Why are you so upset?"

Misty knew why she was so upset. So did Eli and Jared.

"Because...because this is the first I'm hearing of it."

"He's not going to be your stepfather or anything," Dahlia said in a soothing tone. "We were just casually seeing one another. It's not even going on anymore. He's left the company and has a new job."

This was obviously the first that Taylor was hearing about that. Now she was openly pacing, her fingers pressed to her temples.

"When did this happen? Why wasn't I told?"

Frowning, Dahlia stood as well. "Why would we need to tell you? And why are you getting so upset?"

"I'm not upset," Taylor denied, although her body language was telling a different story. "I'm just surprised, that's all. I need to go make a call."

Before Taylor could exit the living room, Eli stepped into the teenager's path. "Wait, I'm not done yet."

"I need to make the call now, Sheriff."

"You can call Tom later, but I doubt he'll pick up the phone," Jared said softly. "He's already moved to Texas with his wife and kids."

"I wasn't–I mean–I don't–"

Tears were welling up in Taylor's eyes and for a moment Misty felt sorry for the young woman.

Just for a moment. Then she reminded herself why they were there.

"What are you talking about, Sheriff?" Dahlia demanded, her own cheeks red. "Tom isn't married with children."

Eli grimaced. "Actually, he is. It was a secret he was keeping from the family, and everyone in town. He had a lot of secrets, didn't he, Taylor?"

The teenager stopped pacing and looked up at Eli, her chin visibly trembling. "I don't–I don't know what you mean."

"I saw you," Misty said quietly. "When I went to the restroom in the downstairs hallway that night. I saw you and Tom."

Dahlia's head whipped around, her sharp gaze now on her daughter. "You and Tom? What were you doing in the hallway with Tom?"

Taylor's mouth opened and closed several times before her words came out like a wail.

"We love each other, Mom. We want to be together."

It was clear that Dahlia didn't have a clue about what her daughter and Tom had been up to. She looked about to faint from shock.

"You love each other," Dahlia repeated, her tone incredulous. "You're too young to be in love with anyone. Did you–did you sleep with him?"

"We love each other," Taylor said again as if her parent wasn't very bright. "I'm going to marry him. I'm going to be his wife."

"Apparently, he already has one of those," Dahlia replied tartly. "Not that he told me that. He told me that he loved me. Did he tell you that too?"

"He did tell me. And I love him too."

There was no confidence like the confidence of a young woman in love. Taylor had pronounced it proudly, full of bravado while Dahlia looked like she wanted to crawl away in shame.

"Then he lied to both of us," her mother said, a few tears falling down her face. "He lied to you and he lied to me. He lied to everyone."

"I have a feeling that someone knew the truth," Jared said, stepping forward. "Taylor, your grandfather knew about you and Tom, didn't he?"

It was a shot in the dark. Misty, Eli, and Jared had talked about this, going around and around and it was the only thing that made any sense. Adam must have known. Somehow. Since he was a man who didn't like modern technology, he must have done it the old-fashioned way with eyes and ears – the staff – all over the estate.

"No–Yes–I mean–"

Taylor choked up, tears streaming down her swollen cheeks, her eyes red.

"He told you to stop seeing Tom, didn't he?" Eli said, stepping closer to Taylor. "Adam knew about you and Tom."

There was a long silence when not one person spoke, the only sounds Taylor's sobs. She'd buried her face in her hands and strangely her own mother wasn't comforting her. Dahlia was crying too but she kept shaking her head as if to deny what was going on right before her eyes. That it couldn't possibly be the truth.

"He told me that morning that he was going to send Tom away," Taylor eventually yelled at the top of her lungs. She was more angry than sad. "He was going to fire him and tell him to leave. He said that if Tom ever came near me again, he'd make sure he didn't work anywhere else ever again. He'd ruin him. I couldn't let that happen."

Here we go.

"So you asked Cara to trade jackets with you that night," Jared said. He didn't pose it as a question because it wasn't. They already knew this for a fact. "You had her drive your brand-new car out of the front gate while you and Brent stayed behind. Somehow you'd convinced him to help you, possibly because he was already mad about his cousin being fired."

Taylor was wringing her hands and chewing on her bottom lip. "No, no, no. That's not how it was."

"We have the video that shows Cara driving out of the front gate," Eli said. "We know that you never left the estate that night, Taylor. Did you and Brent hide somewhere? In the garage, maybe?"

Jared held up the little plastic evidence bag with the button. "This button came from Cara's sweater and we know she wasn't wearing it because she had your jacket on. You were wearing the sweater when you went into your grandfather's study through the French doors. There's a palm print on the window. I'm guessing it will match either you or Brent."

"We hid in the garage."

The words were so soft Misty could barely make them out, unsure she'd heard correctly.

"You hid in the garage," Eli echoed. "And then what, Taylor? You waited for everyone to go to bed?"

"Yes," she nodded. "I watched until the lights all went out, but I knew my grandfather would be up. He likes to work late."

Dahlia came out of her trance and grabbed Taylor's arm, giving it a hard yank. "Shut up. Just shut up. Don't say anything else."

David, who had been unusually quiet, started laughing loudly as if the scene unfolding was utterly hilarious. "For once, it isn't me that's fucked up."

"Shut up, David," Dahlia said angrily. "Just shut up and have another drink."

Her brother reached for the whiskey bottle. "I think I will. This is getting quite interesting."

Dahlia shook Taylor by the shoulders. "Don't say another word, do you understand me? Just shut up."

"Cara and Brent have already given their statements," Eli said, reaching into his back pocket and pulling out a pair of handcuffs. "You might want to call a lawyer, Dahlia. I have to take Taylor in."

"No, not my baby." Dahlia wrapped her arms around Taylor who was fighting off the embrace. "You can't take her."

It was Lydia who stepped forward, insinuating herself between mother and daughter. "Call an attorney, Dahlia. Right now."

"She didn't do this. She couldn't do this," Dahlia said. "She loved her grandfather. He adored her. He would have given her anything."

"He was a mean old man and he thought he could control everyone," Taylor spat out as Eli cuffed her hands behind her. "I'm not sorry he's dead. He didn't care what any of us wanted. He only cared about himself."

David raised his highball glass. "I'll drink to that."

This time it was Lydia who replied. "Shut up, David. No one wants to hear what you think."

He turned his attention to Misty, raising his glass in her direction. "You're lucky you didn't grow up in this house. You would have ended up just like us."

Eli led Taylor out of the house and into his SUV while Lydia helped Dahlia dial her phone. Jared sat down on the arm of the chair Misty was sitting in.

"You know that never would have happened."

"Living in this house?"

He shook his head. "No, turning out like them. There's no way you would have ended up like them. You have far too much heart and compassion inside of you."

She reached for his hand, her strong fingers wrapping around her smaller ones, making her feel loved and secure.

"I have to admit that at the moment I'm glad that Adam ignored me my whole life."

Leaning down, Jared brushed his lips across her forehead. "He never deserved you. You're too good for this family."

Was it better to have no family than a bad one? She'd probably never know the answer to that one. She'd only had a father less than twenty-four hours.

"Thank you for not giving up on this case."

"I'd do anything for you."

He would too. She'd do the same for him. That was family. She might not have grown up in much of one, but she had one now. Jared, the kids, his brothers, and their good friends like Rayne and Dare, Jason and Brinley, Logan and Ava, Reed and Kaylee. And more. People that would always be there whenever needed.

Family wasn't just blood or DNA. It was deeper than that, heart and soul. It was people she'd chosen and trusted. People she could count on and they could count on her. She'd be there for them hell or high water. Family.

And it all started with this man. This amazing, wonderful man that she'd married. He'd helped teach her to trust and to love.

"I love you," she said softly, for no one's ears but his own.

"I love you too. Forever."

It simply wouldn't be long enough.

CHAPTER TWENTY-FIVE

I t was the end of summer. The kids would be going back to school next week and the family would be back in the regular routine of homework and early nights. Lizzie was excited because her best friend was going to be in her class and Nate was lamenting having to go to bed earlier again. Misty had an art showing in the spring. With all of that and the holidays, they'd be as busy as last year and then some.

If someone had asked Jared, he would have said that he preferred the long, languid days of summer where the kids stayed up later and the pace seemed slower. There was more time to play, to read, to interact as a family. In a few years, Lizzie and Nate wouldn't even want anyone to know they *had* parents, but right now they were thrilled to do fun things with Jared and Misty.

His wife had planned one last summer hurrah at the Monroe ranch and had invited everyone they knew. Some were able to make it and some weren't, but it was good to see so many friends and family all together. This had been important to Misty. Since Adam's death she'd been embracing all of their "family" more than she had before. She was right too. These were relationships worth cherishing, nurturing, although she was a hell of a lot better at it than he was.

The kids – and there was a ton of them – were playing in the expansive backyard and there was some screaming and yelling but it was all in fun. At one point, Kyle had put a sprinkler out there and all of them had run through the cool spray, giggling and laughing. There were popsicles too, of course. Ty said it was mandatory.

It was unusually hot for this time of year. It truly was summer's last stand. The weatherman was expecting much chillier weather to come in the next few days and that would be it. Autumn would have arrived.

Dare popped the top on a fresh beer and leaned against the porch railing. He was wearing his usual grouchy expression, but he'd already smiled twice today so Jared had a feeling that his face had pretty much molded in that position. Thankfully, it didn't have a damn bit to do with the man's actual emotions.

"Rayne says that you're trying to recruit the sheriff from that little town that you visited last month."

"Eli," Jared replied. "Good man. Good cop. He'd be an asset to the firm. So would you."

He'd been working on Dare for a while now, but the other man kept saying that he was a small-town cop at heart. Jared wasn't going to give up, though.

Dare chuckled. "I wondered when you'd bring that up. Have you been pushing this Eli just as hard?"

"Not quite. I don't know him as well."

"So the case is all sewn up?" Dare asked. "That was a crazy one."

Dare and their friends didn't even know how crazy. Jared and Misty had decided not to reveal that she'd inherited anything from Adam. Not because they would want any money or anything like that. Their friends weren't the greedy type. But because they still hadn't quite wrapped their minds around the whole thing yet. At some point, they might talk about it. Once they'd decided how they were going to distribute it. Misty was adamant that she didn't want to keep it.

"Will you have to go back for the trial?"

"Probably, we both will. Taylor is going for a self-defense argument."

With a bunch of high-priced lawyers too, courtesy of her mother Dahlia.

Taylor had taken most of their advice when she'd been taken into custody. She'd shut her mouth and hadn't said a word, letting her counsel do it for her. Her story was that her grandfather threatened her and Brent, there had been an argument, and that Brent had picked up the statue and hit Adam on the back of the head.

Brent, on the other hand, had a different story.

He said that he wasn't even in the study when Taylor had picked up the statue and hit her grandfather. He'd been standing outside watching. He'd also said that killing Adam had been all Taylor's idea. She'd roped him in because he was so angry about his cousin. She'd stoked that anger until he was a willing accomplice. They'd hid in the garage that night until everyone had gone to bed and then they'd snuck in the French doors of the study. He'd stayed back while Taylor argued with her grandfather. It was only then that he'd realized that she wasn't as in love with him as he was with her. He hadn't realized that she was seeing Tom.

Angry, he'd threatened to tell on her, but she pointed out that no one would believe him over her because she was rich and pretty. He'd stayed quiet and she'd promised him college money as soon as she received her inheritance. She hadn't known that

Adam had rewritten his will just a few weeks before his death. She hadn't inherited what she'd expected, and she was going to be dependent on her mother.

Brent had also admitted that – at Taylor's behest – he'd fired David's gun to scare Dahlia's horse. Taylor knew that the horses were skittish, and she wanted to make it look like someone had tried to hurt or kill her to make sure that no one suspected her.

He'd also cut the electricity to the garage when Jared and Misty were inside, knowing that the doors would lock. Taylor had started the cars remotely from the house. She'd been trying to scare Jared and Misty away because they were nosing around in the family business.

Taylor's lawyers denied all of this. They were throwing Brent under the bus for most of it. They might just get away with it. Depending on the effectiveness of the lawyers, Jared could see the jury going either way.

Sandra had, of course, been let out of jail. She wasn't talking either as to how she knew to protect Taylor. Jared assumed that she had seen the teenager with Tom and put two and two together.

Dahlia was playing dramatic for the cameras, and David had taken over the reins of the company after twenty-eight days in rehab. The first thing he'd done was give every employee a raise.

Eli said that Lydia was living quietly in San Francisco and trying to stay out of the entire mess while Tom was going for his fifteen minutes of fame. His wife had left him and taken the kids, so now Tom was trying to be a social media star and telling his story to whomever would stand still long enough to listen.

Unlike Taylor or Brent, Cara was going to college this fall but Jared was certain the young woman was going to be called back as a witness in the trial.

"Do you think the self-defense argument is a winner?" Dare

asked.

Jared simply shrugged. "I think this case is going to come down to who has the best lawyers."

"It usually does."

Logan stuck his head out of the back door. "Hey, your wife says to get your ass inside."

"Did she say it just like that or did you take a little creative license?" Jared asked with a chuckle.

"I may have put my own spin on it."

Jared levered out of the chair and excused himself before walking through the back door and into the kitchen. Misty was sitting at the island with his brother Ty and her best friend Rayne. She held up her phone.

"The email came."

They'd been waiting for this. He didn't even have to ask to know what it was.

The DNA results.

He'd pushed it out of his mind these last four weeks, but he'd been aware that Misty hadn't forgotten. She hadn't mentioned it, but she'd written down the date on the calendar that the results were expected. They were two days early. He'd hoped to have figured out how he felt and what he wanted by the time the news showed up.

He hadn't.

Not that it mattered what he wanted. The only thing that mattered was Misty, and in his gut he knew that she wanted Adam to be her father. She wanted connections and that was completely normal even if the family she was connected to wasn't.

"Did you open it?"

Misty shook her head. "I wanted you to be here for that."

Reaching out, Rayne placed her hand over Misty's. "Do you

want to be alone with Jared? We can go."

"No, I want you here." Misty shook her head and reached out her other hand for Jared. He took it, giving it a squeeze. Her skin was so soft. He'd never get tired of doing just this. When they were old and gray, he'd happily hold her hand while they rocked on the back porch. "I want my family with me when I open this."

"It doesn't matter what it says, Mist," Ty said. "You're our sister and we love you. You have lots of family."

Rayne nodded in agreement. "You're my sister and I love you. I'll always be here for you."

Jared was getting choked up and Misty hadn't even opened the email yet.

She took back her hands and thumbed the screen, her fingers visibly shaking. She pulled up the email and read it silently. From where he was standing, he couldn't see what it said.

With a sigh she placed the phone on the table, her features composed. "Adam Reynolds was my father."

It was real now. Before it had only been a possibility but now… It was true.

Sensitive to Misty's feelings, no one said anything for a long time, content to let her deal with it while they stood there to support her in any way she might need them.

"I'm sad that I had so little time to get to know him," she finally said. "But I'm glad that I got to meet him at all. We only had a few hours but I'm grateful for those."

"I think he was grateful too, honey," Jared said, brushing his knuckles against her creamy cheek where a silvery tear was slipping down. "I think meeting you made his last day very happy."

"I hope so. I'm glad that we were there and that you were there to help Eli find who really killed him. I'm glad there was real justice. I'm just kind of sad about what will never be. There was a timer on our relationship from the very first moment. You're so lucky you had so many years with your parents."

I am lucky.

It was a fact that he thought about quite a bit for the rest of the day while he was grilling outside or eating or later telling cop stories with his friends. As the sun set and they all drifted to bed, Jared still sat on the back porch staring out at the starry sky. The air had cooled and he was a bit cold, but he couldn't seem to find the energy to move.

A pair of boots on the plank boards alerted him to another presence. Ty. Holding a bottle of beer.

"I thought you might want another one."

Did he? He'd been careful not to drink too much today. At his age, he didn't recover like he had even ten years ago.

"Why the hell not? Thanks."

Jared accepted the bottle, but Ty didn't move from his spot. Which meant that his little brother had something to say.

"Misty seems okay. I think she's going to be alright."

"She will. It will take time."

"Some things you never get over. Not completely."

Looking up at his brother, Jared had the feeling that the last statement wasn't about Misty at all. It was about him.

"Trying to tell me something?"

"I'm not trying. I just did. You know, it's nights like this that I'll sit outside here and talk to Mom and Dad. I bet they're listening tonight. I bet they really enjoyed the party today. You know how much they loved kids running around."

They had. They had always wanted lots of grandchildren.

Ty had disappeared inside which left Jared all alone. Misty had already gone up to bed. They were staying in the main house while Rayne and Dare and their daughter stayed in Jared and

Misty's home on the ranch.

Talking a long draw from the bottle, Jared didn't even know where to begin. Maybe at the beginning?

"I miss you, Mom and Dad. More than you know. I miss being able to talk to you. You always seemed to have some wisdom for me when I didn't know what to do."

Tears stung the back of Jared's eyes and a stark pain took up residence in his chest just over his heart. Ty was right. Some things you never completely get over. You just learn to move forward.

He'd always miss his parents.

"I get scared sometimes," he admitted, his own voice choked. "I don't deal well with loss. I guess because I don't like to talk about my emotions or show them much. I've been working on that, but I'm still shit at it. I know Misty is hurting too and I should be up there for her right now. Holding her and telling her I love her because I do so much. She's the best thing that's ever happened to me. I'd be nowhere without her. She's given me so much. So much love and trust. My children. Dammit, I wish you were here to see your grandchildren. Mom, I swear Lizzie looks like you when you were young and Nate acts so much like Dad sometimes. He'll get this look on his face and it's just like you, Dad. He's stubborn but he believes so deeply."

His throat had tightened, making speech difficult, but he needed to say all of this. It had been too long.

"I'm sorry I never visit your graves. I just…shit, I just hate it out there. It reminds me that you're gone, and I don't like that. I guess I thought if I pretended that I was fine with you being gone and I ignored it all, that eventually I'd be able to deal with it. But that's not how it works, is it? You taught me so much about life, and now I'm having to learn about death. That's the harder lesson because it's so personal. Losing and loving and still having the courage to do it again and again."

There was nothing but silence in the darkness except for some crickets that were playing a melody. Every now and then there would be a rustle in the trees, but Jared couldn't see anything in the dark. Even if it had been light out, his vision would have been blurred with the tears he couldn't seem to stop. Now that he'd let them loose, they were like a waterfall down his face.

When was the last time he'd cried? The day Nate was born? He hadn't cried the day that Gerald had been placed to rest, although he'd wanted to. He had cried the day that his mother had passed on. He hadn't been able to hold back those tears.

"If it's okay with both of you, I think I'll talk to you every now and then. Don't worry, I won't expect an answer. But it would be nice to have these chats."

And they didn't answer, but damned if Jared didn't sort of feel like his parents were there with him, standing on their own back porch on their own ranch. He could feel them in every corner of this house whether the paint was changed or not. They were a part of the foundation.

This home. This family. This ranch.

It had all been built on the foundation of his parents' love for one another. That would never die or go away, because it had been so real.

I'm their legacy. Me, and Ty, and Royce, and Becky. My family too. Because of us, they'll live forever.

It made everything feel a little less final.

Eventually, he went inside and upstairs where Misty was reading in bed. When she saw him her eyes lit up and her smile widened.

What in the hell did I ever do to deserve her?

"Hey gorgeous, I was wondering when you were going to

join me."

She placed her book on the bedside table and he crawled up the mattress so they were lying side by side, her head on his chest and her long hair tickling his chin. She must have taken a shower because she smelled amazing. He took a deep breath and filled his lungs with her scent, his heart beating a mile a minute.

"I had a few things I needed to do. Are you okay?"

She nodded, her cheek rubbing against his shirt. "I am. I'm sad but having everyone here today really helped me. I'm glad we decided to have this get-together."

"I am too. It was a good idea." He rubbed a silky strand of her hair between his fingertips. "Ty told me tonight that there are some things we aren't meant to get over completely. Do you think that's true?"

"I do. I think I'll always hurt about what might have been with me and Adam. But like I said before, I'm happy that I got to meet him at all. I never thought that I'd meet my father." She sat up on her elbow, their gazes meeting. "What about you? Are you okay?"

"Why wouldn't I be?"

"Because you've been pretending for months that you're fine, but you obviously aren't."

"Were you ever going to say anything about it to me?"

So much for fooling Misty. She was far too smart for him.

"No, because I know you. You'd figure it out eventually."

"I talked to Mom and Dad tonight. You know…when I was outside after everyone left."

She didn't look surprised or shocked.

"That's good. Did it help?"

"Yes. It did. More than I thought it would."

"Then that's really, really good."

Jared was more at peace in this moment than he'd been in a

long time.

"I love you, Misty Foster Monroe. You are without a doubt the most important thing in my life. You and the kids saved me."

Her eyes went all soft and her hand cupped his jaw. "I love you too. We're a family. I never thought I'd ever have one but now that I do, I never want to be without it."

"You couldn't get rid of me if you tried. You can run but I'll always come after you."

"I don't want to run."

"Good, but if you did, I'd just follow you."

Leaning down, she pressed her lips to his until his heart skipped a beat.

"And if you ran, I'd follow you," she said with a soft smile. "We're stuck together, you and I."

That sounded like the closest thing to heaven that he'd ever heard.

Thank you for reading! I hope you enjoyed Hollow Justice. There will be more stories in the Cowboy Justice Association series. Coming soon.

Thank you again for reading.

About the Author

Olivia Jaymes is a wife, mother, lover of sexy romance and cozy mysteries, and caffeine addict. She lives with her husband, son, and two spoiled dogs in central Florida and spends her days typing on her computer with a canine on her lap.

She is currently working on a new cozy mystery series – *A Ravenmist Whodunit* – in addition to her other ongoing romance series.

Visit Olivia Jaymes at
www.OliviaJaymes.com

Made in United States
North Haven, CT
22 September 2023